Danny Womack's .38

Copyright © 2020 Gregory Payette

All rights reserved.

ISBN-13: 978-1-7361465-1-4
Published by 8 Flags Publishing, Inc.

For D.W.S.

Please Join My Reader List

I'd like to invite you to join my reader list to receive free stories, giveaways, and VIP announcements when my new books are released. When you do, you'll receive two free books, *Tell Them I'm Dead* and *What Have You Done?*

Visit **GregoryPayette.com/free-book** to sign up now.

1

DANNY WOMACK STEPPED from his '95 Buick LeSabre and walked across the Raceway gas station parking lot. He pulled open the glass door at the entrance, and the smell of fried chicken escaped past him as he walked inside.

There was already a long line at the counter with mostly blue-collar workers in sweat-stained shirts, hungry from morning work in the hot Florida sun.

Danny sat down on one of four stools at the counter. He reached for the folded newspaper and opened to the front page, scanned over the headlines, then flipped to the obituaries. He gave it a quick glance, folded it and pushed it away.

His friend Jimmy was on the other side of the counter with tongs in his hand. He reached under the yellow lights inside the glass display case and filled a to-go container with fried chicken: two breasts, two drumsticks, and a couple of wings. He covered the chicken with greasy fries and closed the lid on the container, slid it into a white plastic bag and pushed it across the counter. A bead of sweat dripped from his shaved head, down his beard, and landed somewhere on the counter.

Danny stood up from his stool and reached deep into his pocket. He pulled out a handful of loose change and dropped it on the counter. He reached into his other pocket, came out with a couple of crumpled bills. He tossed them on the counter. "Hey, Jimmy, grab me a three-piece, will you? And a Coke. No wings this time."

Jimmy walked alongside the counter and over to Danny. He looked down at the coins and crumpled bills and wiped his forehead with the back of his hand. "I keep working here, I'm going to kill somebody."

Danny didn't say a word.

Jimmy continued, "We gotta come up with something. I can't deal with this shit anymore…"

Danny reached for the newspaper, opened it up and turned it so Jimmy could read it. "You see this?"

Jimmy didn't look down, turned and glanced behind him toward the long line at the register. The metal bell over the glass door rang every half minute as customers piled in. "You think I have time to read the paper?" He walked away from Danny and yelled, "Veronica! Get out here!"

A young woman with pink streaks in her hair—six

inches taller than Jimmy and twice as wide—stepped through a doorway tying an apron around her back.

Jimmy leaned under the hot glass with tongs in his hand. He turned his head and said, "Where the hell've you been?" He straightened himself out and held a piece of fried chicken up in front of him.

She didn't answer him but glanced at Danny and gave him a nod.

Jimmy looked up at the clock over the hood above the deep fryers. "You didn't hear me calling you?"

She pulled her Raceway baseball cap tight over her head and shrugged her thick shoulders. "I was doing something." She stepped behind the register and smiled at the older gentleman on the other side of the register. "Welcome to Raceway."

Jimmy walked over to Danny and put the container of chicken down on the counter. He leaned on his forearm, looked back over his shoulder at Veronica and shook his head.

Danny looked down at the newspaper again and pointed to a picture of a man whose round head took up the entire frame of the photo. "Jerry died."

Jimmy glanced at the paper, then shifted his eyes to Danny. "Russo? He's *dead*? What the hell happened?"

Danny flipped the lid on the container and took out a piece of fried chicken. "Heard he broke into a doctor's home, had a heart attack on the stairs."

Jimmy straightened out from the counter.

"Surprised he made it this long."

Danny took a bite of chicken. With his mouth half-full, he said, "Man taught me a lot."

Jimmy made a face. "Don't give me that sad shit, Danny. He treated you like you were dead even before you went to Raiford." He looked at Veronica serving fried chicken to the long line of people. "You believe all these people? Come to a gas station for fried chicken?"

Danny's mouth was full, but he stopped chewing and looked down at the greasy chicken in front of him. Out of the corner of his mouth, he said, "Where's my Coke?"

Jimmy rolled his eyes and walked away.

The bell over the door rang again. But this time Danny turned and looked, for some reason knew who it'd be.

Carla Weiss—twice his age but sexy with her long, tanned legs and surgically-enhanced breasts pressed up against the inside of her tank top—came up behind Danny and wrapped her arms around him. She kissed him on the cheek. She sat on the stool next to him and grabbed the chicken from his hand, took a bite, and closed her eyes as she chewed. "Mmmm."

He ripped it back from her hand and gave her a look, his eyebrows tight over his eyes. "What the hell?"

She shrugged. "I'm hungry."

He narrowed his eyes and looked straight into hers. "Are you stoned?"

She didn't answer, grabbed the newspaper and looked down at the page. "Why're you reading the obituaries?"

Danny pointed to Jerry Russo's picture. He left a grease spot on it from the tip of his finger. "You see who died?"

She looked down at the paper, then looked up at Danny. "The Michelin Man?"

He nodded and grabbed another piece of chicken from the container. "Heart attack."

Veronica walked over and stood on the other side of the counter. She wiped the sweat from her brow with the back of her wrist and smiled at Carla. "Hey, Carla."

Danny said, "Veronica, get me a Coke, will you?"

Jimmy walked over and brushed past Veronica, already had the Coke in his hand and put it down in front of Danny. He looked at Veronica. "I told you, I'm on the counter today." He nodded toward the two men waiting on the other side of the register. "Go take care of them."

Carla watched Veronica walk away, then turned to Jimmy. "Can I get a tea?"

Jimmy didn't answer, turned and walked back to the deep fryers. He pulled out a metal basket of fried chicken and dumped it into one of the metal pans under the glass.

Carla put her hand on Danny's back. He finished off what was left of his chicken, chewed it all down to the bones and licked his fingers. His eyes were down on the picture of Jerry Russo, the grease stain on top. He looked up at Carla. "I know everyone says he left me hanging… but he taught me a lot. He was a good man, as long as you didn't screw up."

"Was he?" she said, with a look of doubt on her face.

Danny gave her a look. "You didn't know him like I did. He did a lot for me when I was a kid."

"You were a kid. And he skated. You did five years in Raiford and he disappeared."

Jimmy came back with a paper cup, the Lipton tea bag label hanging down over the side. Steam came off the top, and he placed it down in front of Carla. He leaned with one arm down on the counter. "You got any weed?"

She wrapped both hands around the cup and nodded, looked at Jimmy from over the rim.

"Meet me around back," he said.

Carla glanced at Danny. "Be right back." The bell rang when she walked out the front door.

Danny sipped his Coke and turned, watched her through the glass at the front of the store until she disappeared around the corner. She looked good, he thought. Even for a woman twice his age. He turned back and Jimmy was already gone.

Veronica was down the other end in front of the

deep fryers. She said to Danny, "Where'd they go?"

He stared back at her and shrugged but didn't answer. He put his eyes back down on the newspaper and his phone buzzed. He pulled it from his pocket and looked to see who it was; almost put it back in his pocket without answering. But he changed his mind, tapped the screen and brought it up to his face. "Curtis? What's up, man?"

"Where are you?"

"Raceway. Getting lunch."

"Is Jimmy working?"

Danny watched Veronica fill a tray with fried chicken and close the lid over the top. "Yeah, he is."

The call went quiet.

Curtis said, "So I got something I'm working on, if you're still interested in some action."

Danny looked down on the counter at the change and crumpled bills in front of him. "I'm always interested. As long as it's not bullshit. I gotta be careful, so as long as it's worth it."

"I still need to confirm a few things. But there's an old lady, lives out in Riverside. Her estranged husband was an artist... passed away a couple of months back."

"The old lady?"

"No, the husband."

Danny held the phone against his ear and sipped his Coke. "So what else?"

Curtis said, "She got hold of his art after he died.

Had some kind of a battle with the gallery, but the judge said she was the owner... because they never officially divorced."

Danny was confused. "Okay, I guess I'm not following."

"The paintings are worth a few hundred grand. And she goes off to Maine, spends every summer up north."

Danny cracked half a smile. "She's gonna leave the art sitting in her house, waiting for us to take it?"

"Well, that's the part I have to confirm. But I know it's there now. So maybe we won't have to wait."

"Then who cares if she goes to Maine?"

The line went quiet as Danny watched Jimmy come out from the back of the kitchen. The bell rang behind him. Carla walked in and sat next to him, reeking of weed. Danny said, "Curtis, I gotta go. Call me later when you have more details."

2

OFFICER SEAN COYLE stood at the front of the classroom of the Jacksonville Sheriff's Office Academy. He had an image of a .38 Special on the screen behind him and pointed with a laser as he described the firearm.

A young recruit raised his hand. "What's the difference between a .38 and a .38 Special?"

Sean nodded his head. "Good question. But technically, there isn't much of a difference anymore. Smith and Wesson introduced the .38 Special in 1902. And it caught on like wildfire. Most law enforcement officers were carrying .38 Special revolvers, and most of what's out there today is a .38 Special. Although, the truth is, there are other .38s manufactured that aren't technically .38s, but .357s. When we talk about a .38 today it's likely a .38 Special."

The recruit followed up his question. "But it's no

longer a weapon of choice?"

"Remember what I said the other day? It's not a weapon until it's used as a weapon." He pointed with his laser on the screen. "That there is a firearm. And it can be used as a weapon. It's important to make the distinction." He turned back to the class. "You'll still see plenty of these out there on the streets. They're cheap. And they're easy to use." Sean glanced at the clock on the wall. "We can continue this discussion tomorrow."

The recruits stood from their chairs and worked their way to the door on the other side of the room from where Sean stood.

He rubbed his forehead and looked at his watch, even though he'd just looked at the time. He picked up a phone from his desk and saw he had a message from his aunt. It was the second one she'd left within the past hour. He dialed, and she picked up on the first ring.

"Hello?"

"Aunt Nora? It's Sean."

"Are you still coming by? I'm going to be leaving in a few days."

"I know you are." He looked at his watch again. "I'll stop by after I get out of work. Probably by six."

The other end of the line was quiet for a moment. His aunt said, "I haven't been shopping. I don't want to fill up the refrigerator with food that'll go bad."

Sean thought for a moment, knew what she was asking without actually asking. "I'll stop and pick something up. But if there's anything else you need before you go, then—"

"As long as you make sure your friends keep an eye on my house."

"I will. I'll keep an eye on it. I told you that." He turned and looked out the window at the parking lot. "Did you ever call the security company, have the new alarm system installed?"

"I'm not going to pay those thieves. That's all they are. Why would I pay them all that money when my nephew works for the sheriff's office?"

"Well, I'm not on patrol anymore. I just think it's a good idea to have an updated system."

"You just said you'd keep an eye on my house, didn't you?"

"You've got Uncle Joe's artwork lying around. I don't know what you plan to do with it, but—"

"Nobody wants his garbage. I told you that."

Sean rolled his eyes and turned from the window. "I don't think you or anyone else knows what they're worth. But it's better to be safe than sorry."

After a moment, Nora said, "Someone's at my door. I'll see you when you get here."

Sean looked at the screen of his phone and realized she'd hung up. He sat down behind his desk and looked up as Assistant Chief Jeff McDonald walked into his classroom. "Hey, Mac."

Mac stopped and stood across from Sean. "I was thinking about getting a beer. You have plans?"

"I was supposed to take Kim out. But I'm going to have to cancel. My aunt wants me to bring her something to eat."

"She can't feed herself?"

"She's leaving for the summer, doesn't want to attract the rats."

Mac laughed. "Why don't you take Kim over there with you?"

"Are you serious? You only take a woman over to see Aunt Nora when you're trying to end a relationship." Sean turned and looked over his shoulder at the .38 Special still up on the screen. He clicked his laptop and the screen went dark.

Mac said, "You might need to get over that at some point. Especially if they're both going to be around."

Sean gave Mac a look. "I don't know how long either of 'em will be around. But it can wait. If Kim and I are still dating after the summer, I'll introduce her after my aunt's home from Maine. For a few days after her trip she'll be in a good mood… happy to be home in her own bed. But that window's small."

Mac turned and looked over his shoulder at the door, leaned down on Sean's desk with both hands wide from his shoulders. "Keep this quiet, but I've decided to take retirement."

"Retire? No shit?"

Mac nodded. "That's why I thought we'd grab a beer later." He walked to the window, quiet for a moment. He turned to Sean. "I thought maybe I'd put a word in for you."

"A word?"

Mac nodded.

Sean got up and walked around the front of his desk. He leaned back with his arms folded across his chest. "Funny you mention retirement. I've been thinking about a change myself." He looked down at the floor for a moment, then back to Mac. "I think I'm bored."

"Bored?" He stepped closer to Sean. "You got it made here. You're good at what you do. The men you've brought through here over the years have—"

"I want to go back on the street."

Mac raised his eyebrows high on his head, his eyes wide. "Are you serious?" He paused a moment. "Why?"

"I miss the action. I see all these young kids going through here. I remember it, like it was yesterday."

Mac looked at the desks. "Twenty years ago. Me and you… right there in those same seats. Two young dipshits, not a clue what we'd gotten ourselves into."

Sean thought for a moment. "I'm envious, seeing these kids going out there."

Mac laughed. "You're in a good place in your career." He looked Sean in the eye. "And if I do leave—and I don't see why I wouldn't—you'll be in an even better position. Some holes'll open up." He looked at his watch. "I gotta go make a call. Let's keep this conversation between us for now."

3

CURTIS HAD A laptop out on the table at Carla's apartment and turned the screen toward Danny. "This is some of his art from the art gallery where Joseph Reed had his work on display. But that was before his estranged wife took them, got a lawyer to help claim the artwork legally belonged to her."

Danny leaned in closer, looked at the paintings on the website. "Doesn't look like anything special to me."

Curtis gave him a look, then pulled the laptop back and continued scrolling with his finger on the track pad. "Joseph Reed was born in Maine, moved down here to Florida forty years ago. Then, from what I understand, left the wife about ten years back, moved in with his publicist up in New York. But he never divorced his wife. That's how she ended up with the paintings."

Danny leaned back in his chair. "Any kids?"

Curtis nodded. "A daughter. But she doesn't come around here. Lived with the father. Apparently nobody likes the old lady."

"The ex-wife?"

"Estranged. Like I said, they never divorced."

Danny nodded with approval. "You do your homework, huh, Curtis?"

Carla Weiss walked in behind Danny and leaned down with her arms wrapped around his neck. She pushed his long hair aside and kissed him on his unshaven face. She glanced at the screen on the laptop. "I saw this guy's art on the news. It was kind of a big deal around here… a fight over the artwork. His wife started the threats when he was sick, then got her lawyers involved. Sent a crew to the gallery the day he died, pulled the paintings off the walls and drove them straight down here."

Danny pushed Carla's arms from his shoulders and turned, gave her a look. "How come you never said anything about it?"

She shrugged. "You know, I used to be into that stuff. My ex still deals in that world."

Danny turned back to Curtis. "So who's the old lady?"

"Her name's Nora. Nora Reed." Curtis closed the laptop and stood up from the table. "She lives in this big house out in Riverside. Place is practically falling apart, but she's got a lot of money."

Danny narrowed his eyes and stared straight ahead

out the window. He turned in his chair and sat on it backward, facing Curtis in the middle of the kitchen. "So these paintings, you sure they're at her house?"

Before Curtis could answer, Carla said, "There's no way to know what any of it's worth until you have it appraised. Just because it was hanging in some fancy gallery up there doesn't mean it's worth a lot of money." She turned and glanced at Danny. "I could get Charles involved."

Danny pushed her out of his way and looked at Curtis. "Is that true?"

"Is *what* true? That we don't know what they're worth?" He looked at Carla and held his gaze for a moment, then shifted his eyes back to Danny. "I have word, from a pretty reliable source, a couple of his paintings are in the hundred-thousand range."

Danny looked up at Carla and nodded. "Curtis does his homework." He got up from the chair. "You the only one that knows about it?"

Curtis made a face, shook his head. "You kidding? She just said it was on the news. And how do you think I found out? Someone told me. That's why we'll have to move fast. Wait until she goes out of town, someone'll beat us to it."

The door swung open and Jimmy walked in ahead of Veronica. He had a bottle of Jim Beam in his hand and held it up. "Who needs a drink? Got the five-finger discount at Brady's Liquors."

Danny grabbed the bottle from his hand. "How

many times do I have to say it's not worth getting snipped for stealing something costs twenty dollars?" He tapped the side of his head with his finger. "You don't use your brain, Jimmy."

Curtis grabbed it from Danny and looked at the label. "At least take something's a higher quality. Grab a bottle from the Buffalo Trace Antique Collection… seventeen-year-old Eagle Rate. Retails about sixty-five, seventy dollars."

Jimmy grabbed the bottle back from Curtis. "You don't like Jim Beam? Then don't drink it." He shrugged. "Besides, the cameras are on the expensive shit." He turned to Carla leaning against the counter with her arms folded. "You got any glasses?"

Carla gave him a look, then turned and reached into the cabinet behind her. "Who wants a glass?"

Nobody answered, but Veronica stood near the door with her hands in her pockets. "I don't drink that stuff."

Carla looked back at her. "Why're you so quiet? Is everything all right?"

She shrugged her big shoulders and turned her eyes down to the floor. "I'm starving. Jimmy wouldn't stop and let me get something to eat."

Carla gave her a smile. "Maybe you and I can go out, get something to eat. Just the girls."

Veronica turned up a smile as Carla stepped in front of the table, put three glasses down in front of

Jimmy and Danny.

Danny watched Curtis with his back to the rest of them. "You going to have a drink, Curtis?"

Curtis turned, his arms folded over his chest. "Maybe since Nora Reed lives alone we should just go in while she's there. That way, if anything's hidden she'll have to tell us where it is."

Carla shook her head and stared back at Curtis. "You're not going to hurt an old lady, I hope?"

Danny knew the risks of breaking into a home when the owners were present. But Curtis had a point. What if they needed her to talk, tell them where she put the paintings? "Let's see what the security's like first. Keep an eye on the house for a few hours, see who comes and goes." He turned in his chair and looked across the kitchen toward Veronica. "You up for a cable check?"

Veronica nodded. "As long as my uniform still fits. I haven't worn it in a while. And in case you haven't noticed, I've gained a few pounds since working at Raceway."

Danny stared at her for a moment without saying a word, then turned to Carla. "You still have that connection, in case we need a new uniform?"

Carla turned from Danny and smiled back at Veronica. "We'll take care of you, sweetie."

She was the elder in the group, sometimes acted like everyone's mother even though she wanted to seem young. She couldn't help it. Danny wasn't even sure exactly how old she was. Her ex-husband had to've been pushing seventy. Or at least he looked it.

Jimmy shot back his Jim Beam, then tipped the bottle and filled his glass again. He lifted it to Veronica. "Maybe lay off the fried chicken while we're working, you wouldn't have to worry about—"

Danny reached across the table and slapped Jimmy across the side of the head. "Who the fuck are you to talk? Like you're some model of fitness?"

Jimmy straightened out his hair sticking up from where Danny'd whacked him. He shrugged. "Christ, I was just messing around. She says shit like that to me all the time, nobody says a word."

Carla looked at Danny, like she was happy he stuck up for Veronica.

Danny turned in his seat and topped off his glass of bourbon. Everyone was quiet for a moment as he took a sip and turned back to Veronica. "What time are you out of work tomorrow?"

"Eleven. I work the early shift."

Danny turned to Jimmy. "You working?"

Jimmy shook his head with a pout on his face.

Danny said, "The three of us'll go. You drive. I'll see what's inside for security." He looked around at everyone else standing around the kitchen. "I don't care about anything else but the art. That's all we want. I'll see what's stored, what's hanging." He nodded at Curtis. "Can you go over the artwork with me, so I know what to look for?"

Curtis closed his laptop. "You want me to go in… case the place?"

Danny shook his head. "No. I'm going in." He sniffed and turned to Carla.

She lit up a joint from the ashtray next to the sink and took a hit.

Danny said, "You have to smoke that now? We're trying to focus here."

She stared back at him and took another hit. She exhaled and said, "I feel a migraine coming on."

4

SEAN STOOD WITH a white paper bag in his hand outside the front door of his Aunt Nora's hundred-year-old two-story home on Avondale Avenue. He hesitated for a moment, then peeked through the sidelight window along the door and rang the bell.

Anxiety rushed through his veins as the lock clicked on the other side of the door. It was a feeling he'd always get when he'd first show up at Nora's house.

The door opened and Nora stood without saying a word at first. Her eyes went down to the paper bag in Sean's hand. "You didn't get Chinese food again, did you?" She turned from the door without another word.

Sean sighed, stepped inside and closed the door behind him. He walked straight down the hall and into the kitchen, placed the bag down on the counter. "Since when don't you like Chinese?"

Nora was already seated at the round wooden table in the corner of the kitchen. She had a magazine down in front of her. The only noise in the house came from the TV in the other room. She didn't answer his question but looked up from the magazine. "Is that all you ever *eat?* Chinese food?"

Sean stared back at her, but her eyes returned to the magazine. "I'll bring something else next time." He reached inside the bag and pulled out the white paper boxes with the thin metal handles, then reached up into the cabinet for a couple of plates. He turned and placed them both on the table, one right next to Nora's magazine.

Nora picked up a pen and wrote something down on a small pad, then looked up at Sean. "Can't you see I'm doing something?"

He glanced at the clock on the stove and thought about his date with Kim. He regretted he'd canceled. He looked down at Nora's pad. "What are you writing?"

"A list of things I need you to take care of while I'm gone."

Sean looked closer. He didn't like the long list she'd written for him. Not that he minded helping her out. He always did. But Nora was often one to take advantage. He said, "I told you, I have landscapers coming to take care of the lawn."

She gave him a look. "Why would I pay someone

when you can do it for free?"

He turned from her and grabbed a couple of forks and napkins from the drawer, put them down on the table. He pulled open the refrigerator and looked inside. It was empty. "You don't have anything to drink?"

She'd already pushed her pad and magazine aside and started to pick at the beef lo mein she'd shoveled onto her plate. "I told you I didn't have anything. Why didn't you get something to drink?" She took a bite and followed it up right away with another.

Sean said, "You don't leave for two more days, right? You're not going to eat or drink for *two days*?"

She didn't answer, kept her head over her food until it was gone. He watched her dump more rice onto her plate from the white cardboard container.

He ran the glasses under the faucet and carried two glasses to the table. He sat and filled his plate with rice and the General Tso's chicken. He watched Nora shovel more of the food—the food she *didn't* want—into her mouth, like she hadn't eaten in days.

She was seventy-three, with a bitterness to her Sean remembered even back when he was a kid. Especially the time when he got a bike with training wheels. It was his fifth birthday party, and Nora told him he might as well ride a girl's bike if he was going to use training wheels.

"I'll make sure the other officers in the area keep

an eye on your house," he said. "I'll come by when I can. But when I'm at work I'll have to—"

"Come by when you can?" She stopped chewing what was in her mouth and stared back at him from across the table. "I told you, I have some things in here a lot of characters would love to get their hands on. And your uncle's artwork…" She shifted her eyes to the doorway which led to the room with the TV.

Sean wiped his mouth with the thin paper napkin. "I think that's why everyone thought it made the most sense to leave Uncle Joe's art with the gallery, where it was safe."

Nora cocked her head back. "*Uncle* Joe? You haven't seen the man in decades. Don't forget… when he left to go live with that whore up in New York, I'm not the only person he abandoned." She started to take a bite of her food but placed her fork down on her plate. She sat still for a moment and tapped her fingers on the table. "If she had her way, she'd sell every one of them herself. That's the only reason she was ever with him, to one day get her hands on his artwork. I'm sure of it."

Sean sipped his water. "I don't think the gallery would've allowed her to take anything. She wasn't his wife." He used chopsticks to pick up a piece of chicken from his plate, but it dropped onto the table and rolled onto the pad next to Nora. He picked it up with his fingers and stuck it in his mouth.

"Will you just eat with a fork, like a normal American? Why do you think they invented forks? Who needs to eat their dinner with sticks?" She rolled her eyes and shook her head.

Sean smiled at Nora and again used the chopsticks and put another piece of General Tso's in his mouth. He wiped his face with the napkin and swallowed his food. "If you want, I'll call the security company. At least have them make sure the system is working."

She brushed the back of her hand through the air toward Sean. "Those people don't know anything. They want me to pay them all this money every single month. For what? The alarm goes off, anyone with half a brain's going to run."

Sean pressed his lips tight together. "That's not always true."

Nora shrugged. "I don't know anybody who's had their house broken into around here anyway." She picked up her fork and twisted it inside the lo mein.

"I've told you this before: crime has no address. And I don't like the idea they had you on the news when word got around you pulled his paintings from the gallery."

She rolled her eyes. "People around here think Joseph was some kind of a hero, just because he could paint." She took a sip of water and looked into the other room.

Sean said, "Are his paintings still in there, against the wall where you left them?"

Nora nodded.

Sean got up from the table and reached for Nora's plate. "Are you done?" She still had her head turned, looking into the other room. He wondered if her mind had gone somewhere else. She turned back to him. "Leave it alone. I'll clean up."

Sean grabbed her plate and put it with his down in the sink. He walked across the kitchen and into the other room. His eyes went to the baby grand piano in the far back corner by the sliding glass door. It brought back a lot of memories.

Behind it, along the wall, were a dozen paintings. He was about to reach down for one when Nora stepped behind him from the kitchen.

"Don't touch them," she said.

He turned and gave her a look. "I think we need to put these away somewhere, not leave 'em out in the open like this." He turned and looked down at one of the paintings, one of a riverboat—he was sure—out on the St. Johns River. "What about in secure storage? Don't you think that makes sense?"

She narrowed her eyes. "I think you should just mind your own business. That's what *I* think."

Sean shook his head and walked up to the front of the house, thought once she was gone he'd come back and put the paintings somewhere; just get them out of there until she came back from Maine.

He had no idea what they were even worth but figured it had to be something. And now that his uncle was dead, the price had likely gone up. Isn't that how it worked? He looked at his watch and wondered if he still had time to go see Kim. He walked back into the kitchen. "I think I'm going to go. I'll help you clean up and then—"

"I can clean the kitchen. I'm not an invalid, you know."

Sean smiled with a nod. "Will you be here tomorrow?"

"Of course I'll be here. Where else would I go?"

5

DANNY AND VERONICA stepped out onto Avondale Avenue from the white Chevy cargo van in front of Nora's house. Veronica went for the front door and walked up the three brick steps and waited. She held a clipboard in her hand. She wore blue coveralls with a Coastal Cable patch over her left breast. It was tight around her rounded back but did the job. She turned and looked back at Danny.

He walked around the corner of the house with a black bag hung over his shoulder. He looked down at the square plastic cover screwed to the side of the house. He looked out at the van and gave Jimmy a thumbs-up.

Jimmy would call Nora right there, ask her if the technician showed up yet to repair the cable. Veronica would knock on the door.

Danny crouched down in front of the box, ran his fingers along the thick black coax cable that ran from the box and along the side of the house. With a pair of wire cutters he pulled from his bag, he clipped the wire. He put the cutters back in the bag and pulled out a baseball cap with Coastal Cable embroidered on the front. He threw his bag over his shoulder and turned the corner.

Veronica reached for the doorbell.

Danny walked up and stood behind her and the locks on the other side of the door clicked once. Then clicked again.

The door opened. The old woman stood with the phone against her ear. "Yes, sir. They have just arrived now." She looked them both over. "I don't know what the problem is. My TV was working when I had it on a little while ago."

Nora nodded into the phone, then hung it up. "They just called, said you were on your way. I didn't know you'd be here so fast."

Veronica and Danny exchanged a look.

Veronica said, "We're still trying to isolate the issue, but it may be here in your home. If you don't mind, we'd like to come inside to see if we can locate the issue. Hopefully we can get your TV working for you right away."

Nora looked Veronica up and down along her big body—six feet, to be exact—then turned to Danny. "Like I just told the man on the phone, last I checked, my TV was working."

Danny said, "Do you have it on now?"

Nora turned and looked back into her house. "I don't think so."

He said, "Then can we come in and take a look?"

She stared back at him and didn't answer him right away. "For what?"

Veronica broke out her big, friendly smile. "Ma'am, would you mind just checking your TV while we wait here? We wouldn't want to drive away knowing we left one of our best customers without any TV to watch."

Nora shrugged. "I don't watch it much. It's just background noise, as far as I'm concerned. You people charge a lot of money as it is... and there's never anything on worth watching."

Veronica kept the smile on her face. "I understand that. But while you're paying for it, we might as well make sure it's working for you."

"I'm going out of town for a while tomorrow anyway. I usually have it turned off when I go." She put her hand on her chin. "I knew there was something I was forgetting to do." She backed away from the door. "Okay, come on inside." She pointed to the doorway leading into the room just off the foyer. "It's in there."

Danny stepped past her and looked into the room. "Is that your *only* TV?"

Nora nodded. "I told you, there's nothing on. Why would I have more than one TV?"

Danny's eyes went to the television, an older

model that must've been at least twenty years old. "That's a classic," he said with a laugh. He stepped in front of the TV and looked back at Nora. "You have a remote?"

She looked around the room, then turned and disappeared through another doorway and into her kitchen.

Danny looked at the baby grand piano at the back of the room, just to the right of the sliding glass doors. The room stretched from the front to the back of the house, with hardwood floors covered by a long Oriental rug. He gave Veronica a look, then nodded toward the framed paintings on the floor, leaned up against the wall behind the piano. There was a white sheet on the floor underneath them.

Nora came back through the doorway.

Veronica nodded toward the piano. "You play piano, ma'am?"

Nora stepped around the mahogany coffee table in front of the orange velvet sofa and pulled open a drawer. She turned back to the sofa and reached between the cushions, came up with the remote in her hand and handed it to Danny. She looked up at Veronica. "My husband used to play."

Danny clicked the remote and turned on the TV. With his eyes on the screen, he said, "He's not home?" He glanced back at Nora.

"My husband?" She shook her head. "Son of a bitch is dead." Her eyes went to the paintings on the floor.

The TV was on but had *No Signal* in green lettering across the screen.

Danny reached around the back of the TV, pretended to do something, then shook his head. "This one looks okay from here." He looked back at Nora. "Mind if I look around at the other outlets in the house?"

Nora shook her head. "I told you, it's my only TV."

Veronica looked down at the clipboard. "We just need to check the other outlets coming into the house. Even if a TV isn't connected."

Danny walked around the perimeter of the room, ran his eyes along the floor. He stepped behind the piano and looked down at the paintings. Right away he recognized one from the website Curtis showed him.

Veronica said, "Would you mind showing me the other rooms?"

Nora seemed to hesitate a moment but then walked down the hall. Veronica followed.

Danny used his phone and pulled each painting forward. He took as many photos as he could.

Nora walked up behind him. "What do you think you're doing?"

Danny turned and slid the phone back into his pocket. "Oh, I'm sorry. I saw these paintings, I was trying to see behind them... make sure another outlet wasn't covered."

She stared at him for a moment with her hands on her hips but didn't say anything else.

Veronica walked back into the room, looked and mouthed, "I'm sorry," to him.

He walked to the front door, then turned with his hand on the knob. "Well, everything seems okay in here. I'm going to have a look at the connections outside." He glanced at Veronica. "Did you check the upstairs outlets?"

She shook her head. "We were about to…"

Nora said, "Do you really need to look upstairs? I don't know if I like strangers going into my bedroom."

Danny shrugged. "Well, I'd hate to ignore any possible issues. Especially if there's a fire hazard of some sort."

"A *fire hazard?* From *what?*"

"Well, even though it's just cable TV, there's still an electrical current." He pulled open the door. "Ma'am, if you'd just let her have a look in all the rooms, we'll be out of your hair in no time... let you get back to whatever you were doing."

Danny walked outside without another word and walked around the corner. He pulled out his crimping tools and stripped the cover from the cut line, capped each end and connected them back together.

6

SEAN WALKED ACROSS the parking lot of the training academy toward his Ford Explorer. He turned when he heard the roar of Mac's refurbished 1974 Dodge Charger behind him.

Mac bought the repo'd muscle car from the auction and paid thirty-four hundred dollars for it. A steal, as Mac liked to say.

Sean wasn't much into cars himself. He just needed wheels to get him around, and nothing more.

Mac backed the rear end into the parking space next to Sean's Explorer. He rolled down the window and Journey's "Don't Stop Believing" poured from the speakers inside his car. He lowered the sound and looked out at Sean. "What are you doing for lunch?"

Sean stopped and leaned against the side of the Explorer with his arms folded in front of him. "I was just going to grab a salad over at—"

"Salad?" Mac laughed and nodded his head toward the passenger side. "Get in. I'm craving fried chicken."

Sean looked over the roof of the car. "Fried chicken? I was thinking of something a little more healthy."

"You're the last person who has to worry about that." Mac waved him inside. "Come on. We'll take a ride out to Raceway in Murray Hill. Best fried chicken in Jacksonville."

Sean thought a moment then walked around to the passenger side. He stepped inside the Charger. "Best fried chicken in Jax, huh?"

Mac pulled out of the parking space. He revved the engine and glided through the parking lot. "I've never taken you to Raceway."

Sean gave him a look, wasn't sure if he was joking or not. "The gas station?"

Mac turned to him and smiled with a nod. "Everybody knows about Raceway."

"Fried chicken... from a gas station?" Sean turned and looked out the passenger-side window.

Mac laughed, his eyebrows up high on his head. "You'll see what I mean." He hit the gas and ripped the car out onto Capper Road, made a couple of turns and took 104. He looped around onto 295, headed south with the engine screaming. He hit about eighty-five as he merged into the lane.

Sean pushed the seat back to give his long legs a

little more room. "I wanted to talk to you about what I said to you yesterday."

Mac glanced at him, his face a bit perplexed. "Which part?"

"Me going back on patrol."

"I wasn't sure if you were serious. I thought after I told you I was retiring, you might…" He stopped and glanced over at Sean. "You're serious?"

Sean tried to nod, but his head kicked back against the seat as Mac downshifted and passed a couple of trucks on the right.

"I don't have kids to worry about. And, of course, I'm not married."

Mac slowed down a little closer to the speed limit, his eyes on the road. "What about Kim?"

"What about her? I don't know… it's not that serious. We both have our own lives. The truth is, I've been thinking about it for a while. I could be out there really helping people, making a real difference."

"You make a difference already. You're one of the best instructors we have. The recruits love you… and the academy wouldn't be what it is today if you weren't as involved as you are. I know you like to think you're not getting up there in age. But it's a young man's game."

He stared straight ahead. "I'm barely forty."

Mac shrugged. "I'm forty-four… and I'm retiring. And nobody's going to change my mind."

They both drove quiet for the next couple of miles

until Mac pulled off the highway, turned on Cassat Avenue. He pulled into the busy Raceway parking lot, found a spot out front.

Sean said, "We're not doing the drive through?"

Mac pushed open the driver's side door and stepped out. "You think I want my car smelling like fried chicken?" He walked up to the door and held it open for Sean to walk in ahead of him.

The line was long inside but moved fast. Sean couldn't help looking at the man and woman seated at the counter at the far end from where the fried chicken was served. He was sure he recognized the woman. She was older than the man, although he had an aged look about him, like he'd been around awhile.

Mac stepped to the register.

"Welcome to Raceway," the young woman said from the other side of the counter. She glanced from Mac to Sean. "How may I help you two officers?"

Mac ordered a seven-piece with fries and turned to Sean. "You want the same thing?"

Sean looked up at the menu on the wall, then shook his head. "Just a three-piece. White meat. I'll get a Coke with it."

Mac said, "No fries?" He looked down as Sean pulled out his wallet. "Put that away. It's my treat." He turned to the woman and smiled. "I told him this place has the best fried chicken in Jax. He doesn't believe me."

Her eyebrows went high on her head, and her eyes opened wide. She looked at Sean as she nodded and ran the back of her wrist across her damp forehead. "It's true. Best around." She turned and filled the white containers with chicken and handed them to Mac over the counter. She gave them two empty cups and nodded toward the soda dispenser against the opposite wall. "Drinks're over there."

They got their drinks and walked to a table in the back corner.

Sean looked at his watch. "I don't have that much time, you know."

Mac lifted the top of his container and shoved a fry in his mouth, leaned over and grabbed a chicken leg then ate around the bone before Sean had even sat down. "Don't worry, I'll get you back on time."

Sean pulled out a chair and sat across from Mac. "Kim wasn't happy I canceled on her last night. I think it might be over for good this time."

Mac dug back into the foam container for another piece of chicken. "That's too bad. All for another joy-filled night at Nora's?"

Sean picked up a piece of chicken, held it in front of him before he took a bite. "And you know what she said?"

"Kim?"

"No, my aunt. She told me I'm not a real cop." He bit into the chicken. "Can you believe that?"

Mac laughed. "Is that why you want to go back on the streets? So your aunt will respect you?" He shoved another french fry in his mouth, nodded at the Glock 22 in Sean's holster. "You show her that? Tell her you're as much an officer of the law as anybody…"

Sean wiped the grease from his mouth and his fingers with the thin napkin from the chrome dispenser. He reached for his Coke and took a sip.

"So what do you think?" Mac said. "Good chicken, isn't it?"

Sean took another sip of soda and thought for a moment. "You think I'm being a fool?"

Mac picked a piece of meat off the bone between his fingers, flipped it in his mouth, and leaned back in his chair. "I think you forget why you left, or blocked it out of your head somehow."

"But you know it was never my choice."

Mac stared back at Sean. "You had plenty of people on your side. And if you wanted to go back out on patrol, you *could* have. But you and I both know, you chose the best option at the time. Like I said, you've been good for the academy." He reached down into the container and pulled out another piece of chicken.

Sean had a snarl to his lip, watched Mac plow through his seven pieces of chicken. "Aren't you full?"

Mac looked down at his stomach hanging over his

belt. "Does this thing look like it'll get full off a few pieces of chicken?" He shook his head and took another bite, sucked the meat clean off the bone.

Sean picked at his food, then looked up at the clock above the menu on the wall. "Hate to rush you, but I should get back."

They both got up from the table. Sean barely ate, tossed what was left in the garbage and headed for the door.

They stepped outside and Mac turned and looked through the glass door toward the young woman behind the counter. "You know who that was? The big girl?"

Sean looked back, then rolled his eyes. "I don't think a young woman wants to be described as a 'big girl.'" He stood outside the passenger side of Mac's car and pulled on the handle. "But, no, I don't know who she is."

Mac nodded, looked at Sean over the roof. "That's Veronica Hobson. Her father's Walt Hobson."

"Chief Hobson? From the Fernandina Beach PD?"

They both ducked inside the car. Mac turned to him and nodded. "Yeah. His daughter."

Sean looked ahead through the windshield and inside the gas station through the glass door. He could see Veronica leaning on the counter across from the two people on the stools. "He still in jail?"

Mac nodded. "He's got another three to go."

7

JIMMY TURNED TO Danny from the passenger seat. "I just don't understand why you brought Veronica to the old lady's with you. She stands out like a sore thumb, and half the sheriff's office knows who she is."

Danny turned into the parking lot of the 7-Eleven without looking over at Jimmy. "Last time I took you in to case a house you got into an argument with the owner. Guy called the cops." He pulled into the parking space and looked at Jimmy. "Why does it matter? We know exactly where the paintings are." He pulled into a space in front of the ice freezer and turned off the ignition. "Hurry up, will you."

The passenger door creaked when Jimmy pushed it open. He stopped before he stepped out and turned to Danny. "You got any cash?"

Danny took a deep breath and exhaled before he answered. He shook his head and looked down at his fuel gauge. "I'm on E. I need whatever I have for gas." He looked up at the sign on the corner of the lot. "And it's five cents cheaper down the street." Danny started the car and dropped it into reverse but kept his foot on the brake. "Close the door, will you?"

Jimmy gripped the top of the open window. "I thought we were getting some beer?" He stepped out of the car and turned, ducked his head down and looked at Danny. "And I need a pack of smokes."

"But you don't have any money?"

Jimmy straightened out and reached deep into his pocket. He pulled out a couple of bills and a handful of change. "You don't have a ten?"

Danny shook his head. "I'm on empty. Come on, close the door."

Jimmy stared at Danny and slammed the door closed. He ducked down again and looked in through the open window. "Keep it running."

"Jimmy, wait!"

But Jimmy didn't look back and walked inside the 7-Eleven.

Danny looked up in his rearview and looked around at all the cars in the lot, two at the gas pumps and a white van a few spots away. "Shit," was all he said as he backed the Buick out and turned it so he faced the road. He parked along the sidewalk and blocked the first two empty parking spaces. He slammed the heel of his palm against the steering wheel three or four times. "Shit! Shit! Shit!" He looked over his shoulder at the entrance to the 7-Eleven and saw the glass door fly open. Jimmy ran out and yelled, but Danny couldn't hear what he said.

He already had the car in drive and his foot on the brake. Jimmy opened the door and Danny hit the gas.

Jimmy threw a white plastic 7-Eleven bag on the floor. Two cartons of Marlboro Golds fell out next to an eighteen pack of Budweiser. Jimmy tried to hang on with the door still open.

Danny hit West Union. The tires squealed.

Multiple popping sounds rang out from behind them. Danny and Jimmy both ducked their heads. The rear window exploded.

Jimmy was almost on the floor between the dash and the passenger seat. "He's shooting at us!"

Danny had the pedal to the floor and yelled over the screaming wind inside the car. "*No shit!*" He looked up in the rearview. A man with a rifle stood out in the middle of the street and fired off another two shots. But Danny yanked the wheel and turned onto North Main. He slapped his foot down on the pedal as far as it would go.

"*Jesus Christ, Jimmy!* You can't just pull out your .38, go hold up a goddamn 7-Eleven 'cause you're thirsty!" He shook his head and slammed his palm over the steering wheel. *"You just can't do that shit.* You wonder why nobody trusts you to do anything?" He looked in the rearview at what was left of the window behind him.

Jimmy reached down for the plastic bag on the floor, pulled out a handful of cash. "Quit your whining. I got you some gas money."

Danny stared at the cash, shifted his eyes back to Jimmy. "Only fools hold up convenience stores. Especially in broad daylight... people all around."

Jimmy held up the cash. "Man in front of me paid with a hundred-dollar bill. Or I wouldn't have thought of it."

Danny rolled his eyes. "We gotta get this car off the road. I don't know how much gas is left, and the cops'll be looking for us. Like I need this? We got bigger fish to fry than stealing a hundred bucks."

Jimmy laughed. "Shit, I got more than a hundred. All I said was the hundred-dollar bill gave me the idea."

Danny reached for the cash from Jimmy's hand, squeezed it into a ball, then opened his hand over Jimmy's lap. The cash blew all over the place. "It ain't worth it. That's all I'm sayin'."

Jimmy moved around, grabbed whatever bills he could before they blew out the door and stuffed them back in the plastic bag. "It's more than I make serving fried chicken at a gas station."

Danny had his eyes in the rearview, making sure

nobody was coming after them.

Jimmy said, "Oh shit."

Danny turned and looked straight ahead at a Jacksonville sheriff's vehicle, coming from the northbound side of the Main Street Bridge. He looked down at his speedometer and eased his foot off the gas. He turned to Jimmy. "You look at the cameras in there? Good chance they got a shot of you. I hope you know that." His heart pounded as the sheriff's vehicle got closer.

They were both quiet, stared straight ahead and started across the bridge. The vehicle went past them on the other side of the bridge, heading north. Danny turned to Jimmy. "Don't pull that shit again. Damn near had a goddamn heart attack."

Jimmy let out a howl. "You gotta relax."

Danny had his eyes back in the rearview. "Oh shit..."

The sheriff's vehicle made a hard one-eighty and changed direction at the end of the bridge, turned southbound... about a couple hundred yards behind Danny and Jimmy.

Danny looked down at the gas gauge and exited the bridge. He cut over to Independence. His eyes were focused on the road but he glanced in the rearview. The lights of the sheriff's vehicle were still in the distance. But getting closer.

He turned down 90 and just past Treaty Park, turned into the Hampton Inn parking lot and drove around back.

Jimmy looked back. "We lose him?"

Danny didn't answer, but said, "She."

"She? How'd you know that?"

"Because I saw her when we passed on the bridge." Danny wanted to pull the .38 from Jimmy's pants and stick it against Jimmy's skull, make sure he knew how stupid he was. But he threw open the door and stepped outside, walked across the parking lot until the smell of Jimmy's cigarette was far enough away.

8

SEAN WALKED PAST an old convertible BMW 325i with a torn leather roof and faded gray paint. The hood didn't match. The New York plates got him thinking as he continued up the driveway of his aunt's house.

He rang the doorbell and glanced back at the Beemer. The locks clicked on the other side and the door opened. Nora stood in the doorway, her hand on the edge of the door.

Sean noticed a look on Nora's face he hadn't seen in quite some time. She was smiling. Sean wondered if it was really his aunt or if someone had taken over her body.

Sean pointed behind him with his thumb toward the BMW. "Who's that?"

Nora showed off her white, porcelain-capped teeth as she backed off from the doorway. "You'll never believe it."

Sean walked in behind her and looked into the first room on the left with the TV on, but the volume down. He stepped to the back of the room near the sliding glass door.

A young woman sat on the couch.

Nora held her hand out and gestured with her fingers for Sean to come closer. "You remember Gracie, don't you?"

Sean didn't say a word. Not right away.

Gracie sat with a smile, in her open-toed sandals and jeans torn at both knees, like she was still a kid. The Grateful Dead T-shirt topped it off. She worked hard to get that look, even back when she was a kid.

She looked up at him from the couch and smiled. "It's been a long time, Sean."

He took a moment, glanced at Nora, then turned back to Gracie and nodded. "Yes. It has." He narrowed his eyes. "So what brings you back?"

Nora interrupted, "I was just telling Gracie I don't have much food, thought maybe you'd pick something up if we ordered in. Maybe Chinese?"

Sean turned and gave Nora a look. He opened his mouth to remind her she complained about the Chinese food he brought the night before. But he let it go.

Gracie stood up from the couch and stretched her back. "Any good pizza around? I'm sure nothing like New York, but..." She shrugged, her hands in her back pockets. "I guess I'm a little spoiled."

Nora walked past Sean and through the doorway into the kitchen. "Let me get my purse. I'll give you some money if you want to run out and grab a pizza we can have for lunch?"

"I have to get back to work. I just stopped by to tell you I found someone to cut the grass while you're in Maine."

Nora shook her head. "I've been cutting it myself for as long as I can remember." She turned to Gracie. "Ever since you and your father left..."

Gracie sat back down on the couch and cracked her knuckles. She leaned forward with her elbows on her knees, her eyes down on the floor. "I was thinking..." She raised her eyes toward Nora. "Maybe I can stay here and watch the place while you're away?"

Nora looked like she wanted to force a smile but it wasn't going to work. She looked at Sean, then turned and walked through the open doorway into the kitchen. "Let me go find my purse."

Sean looked around the room, watched Gracie's eyes gazing at the paintings up against the wall behind the baby grand, just a few feet away.

Nora walked back in the room and handed Sean a ten-dollar bill. "You can go to Ronnie's. It says *New York*-style pizza, but I don't know the difference. I guess nobody sells *Florida* style, whatever that would be..."

Gracie looked back and forth between Sean and

Nora and laughed. "I think it means it would be too hot."

Nora and Sean exchanged a look, but neither cracked a smile.

Nora walked out of the room again without a word.

Gracie, again, stood from the couch and walked over to Sean. She took the money from his hand. "If you have to get back, I'll go pick it up."

She started for the door, but Sean stepped in front of her. "What is it you want, Gracie? You show up after all these years... you must have a reason."

"Sean, I just—"

"Save it, Gracie. I've taken care of your mother for all these years. I don't even know how long it's been. When was the last time you called?"

"That's not true. I've..."

"You've left messages when you knew she wouldn't be home."

Gracie opened her mouth to talk but stopped. "I..." She scratched her forehead, like she did when she was a kid, when she was caught doing something wrong or had something to hide. She looked Sean in the eye. "Does she know?"

He waited a moment before he answered. "That you did time at Bedford Hills?"

Gracie looked toward the kitchen, then gave him a look. "Shhhh."

Sean shook his head. "I never told her a thing. It

wouldn't have done her any good." He looked down at the paintings. "She always made excuses for you."

Gracie stared back at him but didn't say a word.

"So what's the matter, Daddy's not around to take care of you?" He looked around, made sure Nora wasn't listening. "You're back down to see what you can get out of her?"

Gracie shook her head. "I hardly spoke to my father the last few years. He was pretty upset when I got arrested."

Nora turned the corner with a coupon in her hand. "Here's a dollar off a pizza at Ronnie's." She looked at the front and back. "I don't know if it's still good." She looked at Gracie. "Tell Sean whatever you'd like, so he can get it before he goes back to work."

Gracie held up the ten-dollar bill she took from Sean and grabbed the coupon from Nora's hand. "He has to go back to work now. I'll go pick it up." She turned to the sliding glass door at the back of the room, then looked at Nora. "Maybe we can eat outside... and catch up?"

Sean walked out the door with Gracie and nodded at her BMW. "I'm surprised your Beemer made it all the way down here."

She walked down the driveway. "Still runs."

Sean stopped and looked inside her car. "I

remember when your father bought this thing. Brand new. He'd hit the big time after all those years of struggling." He shook his head. "Then takes off on the woman who stuck by his side all those years." He gave Gracie a look. "I don't know what made you choose him over your own mother."

Gracie looked toward Nora's house—the same house she grew up in. "You're the only one who pretends she's not crazy." She stared back at Sean. "You don't know what it was like. Even when I was young. She abused my father."

"Is that what he told you?"

Gracie shook her head. "I was there. She was mean to him."

They kept a stare on each other for a moment, then Sean continued to his Explorer parked on the street. "You don't abandon your own mother, Gracie." He pulled open his door and looked up at her, standing in front of her car watching him. "And now you're back with your hand out because Daddy didn't leave you shit."

9

DANNY PARKED THE Buick in a friend's garage until he could figure out what to do with it, knowing the cops likely knew what car to look for. Carla picked him up, and together they went back to her apartment.

They sat on the couch next to each other, the sun reflecting off the glass coffee table in front of them. Carla played with the hair on the back of his head with one leg up on his thigh.

Danny stared straight ahead. "I don't know what to do about Jimmy. He's a loose cannon."

"You give him too many chances, if you ask me. For such a badass, sometimes you're too nice, get taken advantage of. And you don't even know it." She slid her hands through the buttons on his short-sleeved shirt and rubbed his chest.

He turned to her and she smiled, biting her lower lip.

She looked into his eyes. "Sometimes, it's all right to let someone take advantage of you." She slid over and straddled him, both hands around his neck and her legs locked behind his back.

Danny stared straight ahead almost as if he were looking through her. He pushed her off and stood up from the couch. "I either have to give him a role where he's barely involved, make him think he's doing something more... or tell him straight out we're going to do it without him." He looked down at Carla. "After this last stunt..." Danny walked over to the window and looked out into the sun. "I can't even drive my own goddamn car until I'm sure the sheriff's office has given up looking for it."

Carla walked over and stood behind him, put on her best Southern charm even though she grew up in New York. "I know that was your nana's car and all... but I can't see a point in time where you can drive it down the road without being worried every time you pass a sheriff's vehicle."

He turned to her. "I trust that car more than I trust Jimmy at this point."

Carla stepped toward him, wrapped one arm around his neck and slid the other down the front of his pants.

Danny and Carla were naked in her bed. Danny stared up at the ceiling with one hand behind his head as Carla smoked a cigarette and flipped through the *Southern Living* magazine.

Danny heard the sound of a key in the door out front. He sat up and turned to Carla, who didn't seem to notice. "Someone else have a key to this place?"

Carla shook her head.

Danny leaned over and opened the drawer in the side table next to him, grabbed his .38 Jerry Russo gave him when he was just fifteen. He placed the gun down on the bed and pulled on his jeans from the floor, grabbed the gun and held it with his finger near the trigger. He stepped to the doorway and turned to Carla, put his finger up to his lips and stood behind the door with his back against the wall.

Carla got up, hurried across the room and into the bathroom a few feet from where Danny stood. She left the door open but stayed back out of view.

The door to the apartment opened and closed.

A voice from the other side of the wall said, "Carla? You here?"

Danny glanced at Carla as she poked her head out of the bathroom doorway. He gave her a look. He kept his voice hushed. "Who is it?"

She shrugged at Danny, then out loud she said, "Yes? Who is it?"

The voice said, "What do you mean 'Who is it?'"

Carla walked past Danny and pushed his gun down by his side. "Put that away," she said. She wrapped her robe tight around her waist and started into the other room. "It's my ex-husband."

Danny tucked the cold gun into his waistband, stepped to the bed and grabbed his shirt off the floor and threw it over his back. He left it unbuttoned, showing off his six-pack abs.

He walked out to the living room and looked at Carla's ex-husband, short and plump, with his white hair slicked back on his red balding head.

Carla said, "Danny, I'd like you to meet my ex-husband, Charles. Charles, this is Danny."

Charles's eyebrows went high up on his head, his eyes wide open. He gave Carla a look. "Jesus Christ, Carla. He's just a kid." He turned and pulled open the refrigerator, looked inside for a moment, then closed it. He gave Danny a nod. "You like the cougars?"

Danny stared back at him but didn't say a word as he looked from Charles to Carla. She was at least a head taller than Charles. And much better looking. Somewhere in her upper forties, she didn't look her age. Maybe thirty-eight. Either way, Danny couldn't picture them together. Although twenty years ago, maybe it was different.

Carla folded her arms across her chest and looked down at Charles. "Just because you own the building, doesn't mean you can just come in and out of my apartment whenever you want." She stood by his side.

Charles shrugged. "I was just checking up on you." He nodded toward Danny. "Looks like Danny-boy's taking care of you. At least, as best he can. Right, Danny?" Charles gave him a smirk.

Danny thought maybe he'd knock it right off his face. "I know who you are," he said, the first words out of his mouth since he walked from the bedroom.

Charles pulled a chair out from under the kitchen table and sat down. He stared back at Danny. "You do, huh?"

Danny nodded. "You knew Jerry Russo."

Charles's face brightened up. "The Michelin Man? You know Jerry?"

"I used to work for him. You helped us flip some artwork, maybe some jewelry. Am I right?"

Charles glanced at Carla, then gave Danny a nod. "Small goddamn world, isn't it?"

Carla looked back and forth between Danny and Charles.

Charles looked up from the table. "So how'd you end up here, banging my ex?" His eyes shifted to Carla, and he gave her a wink. "You're a good-looking kid. But you're probably, what, half her age?" He shrugged. "Not that Carla can't keep up with a youngster like yourself."

Danny's mind was going somewhere else, thinking about the paintings at Nora Reed's house. He thought maybe Charles was the missing link in

Danny's plan. "You're still in the business?"

Charles glanced at Carla, held his gaze for a moment. He got up from the table and scratched his head. "I fly under the radar now, more than I used to." He gave Carla a nod. "Carla knows that..."

Danny hesitated a moment, glanced at Carla, then shifted his eyes back to Charles. "We have a job coming up involving some high-value artwork... supposed to be worth quite a bit of money."

Charles squinted his eyes. "I need to be careful who I work with nowadays. I did six years in state. And when you come out, you're like a duck with a clipped wing. Got an orange tag on your foot. You know what I mean? They've always got an eye on you... watching all the ponds, see where you swim."

Danny said, "I did a couple years myself. Raiford."

Carla walked up to Charles and grabbed him by the arm. "Why don't we talk about this later." She pulled open the door and guided him out into the hall. "Next time, make sure you knock before you come in my apartment."

He put his hands up in front of him. "Whoa, Carla. Hang on a minute, will you? Can I at least hear more about this so-called opportunity?"

Carla shook her head. "No, not now. I'm not sure I like the idea of you two being involved in something like this together."

Danny had his eyes on Carla. "Why's it up to you to decide?"

Charles stepped in from the hall and looked at Danny and smiled. "That's right, kid. Don't let her push you around. That's what she does. She's very controlling."

Carla pushed Charles back out the door. "Get out. We'll call you if we need you." She slammed the door behind him, then turned and walked past Danny and into her bedroom.

10

SEAN SAT IN Mac's office watching him on the phone from the other side of the desk. Mac held up his index finger, nodded his head, then flipped his hand. He gave Sean a thumbs-up.

Mac smiled into the phone. "No, I'm not sure he knows exactly what he's getting himself into. But he'll find out soon enough. You and I both know he's one of our finest." Mac stared back at Sean, the phone up against his ear. "He'll be very happy to hear that. And I appreciate you helping him out." Mac put down the phone and looked down at his hands folded in front of him. He lifted his eyes to Sean and smiled. "Captain Ward is clearing a desk for you." He stood and stretched his hand out to Sean. "Congratulations. Looks like you got your wish... if that's what I can call it."

Sean nodded as he shook Mac's hand but didn't speak right away as a mix of emotions ran through his mind.

Mac sat back down behind his desk. "You don't have anything to say?" He smiled.

"I didn't expect it to happen so fast. I'm in shock."

Mac shrugged. "Timing's not bad. It's the last week of training for the graduating recruits. And I'm going to be sitting my ass on a beach somewhere for what'll hopefully be the last time I retire."

"Yeah, until you get bored."

Mac shook his head. "Me? I don't have whatever it is you have inside you. I know how to relax... enjoy life."

Sean smirked. "I'll make sure they don't give away your parking space too soon."

"Don't get your hopes up. But I'll be sure to send you a postcard."

Sean leaned forward in the chair, his elbows on his knees. He looked down, studied his hands and thought how they looked different. His skin had aged. He looked up at Mac. "You think I'm crazy?"

Mac shrugged. "What the hell's it matter what *I* think? But don't go questioning this now... you've got yourself the fresh start you were looking for. Captain's already got you set up with..." Mac paused a moment. "You remember Officer Cash, don't you?"

"Jenna Cash?"

Mac nodded. "She's about ten years younger than you, but she'll be guiding you through the world over there in zone four."

"Zone four? I thought—"

"At your age…" Mac shuffled some papers on his desk. "Not a bad place to get acclimated."

"So much for the action," Sean said.

"Hey, but look at the added bonus. You'll be able to keep an eye on Aunt Nora's house." Mac stood from his desk and opened his office door.

Sean got up and shook Mac's hand as he stepped out into the hall. "Is there any reason I need to keep this quiet?"

Mac shook his head. "Might as well tell your recruits they'll be seeing more of you than they might like."

They both stepped from Mac's office and headed down the hall.

Sean looked at the framed photos hung on the wall, each of an officer killed in the line of duty. He stopped and gazed at what looked like nothing more than a young boy, barely old enough to be out of high school. The name Brian Wilson was etched into the gold plate below his black and white photo. The date said 1967… the same year the Duval County Sheriff's Office merged with the Jacksonville Police Department.

Mac was a few steps ahead and Sean hurried to catch up with him. "Do you remember my cousin Gracie?"

Mac gave Sean a look. "Gracie?" He nodded. "Of

course. She must be, what, forty-something by now?"

Sean shook his head. "Thirty-six."

"She still in jail?"

Sean stopped at the door and looked inside his classroom. The recruits were already seated at their desks. He turned to Mac. "She's back in Jax. Staying at her mother's house." He took a step into the classroom, then turned back and reached out to shake Mac's hand. "Thanks again, Mac."

Mac looked around the hall as a couple of recruits walked past them and stepped into the classroom. He turned back to Sean. "Maybe you should wait a few weeks before you thank me. You might be cursing my name, wondering why I didn't try to talk you out of it." He gave Sean a crooked smile, then walked away.

"Have some faith, Mac."

Mac held up his hand and gave a thumbs-up without looking back, then disappeared around the corner.

Sean stepped into his classroom and walked to his desk. He looked around the room at the recruits, most of them at least twenty years younger than him. "Morning, everyone."

"Morning, sir."

"I want to make an announcement. This will have little impact on you, since we only have a few more days. First, I want to tell you how much I've enjoyed being your instructor, watching you all grow. It wasn't that long ago I was in those exact chairs, looking up at what I thought, at the time, was an old man. He was barely forty." Sean looked down at the floor. "I came off the streets to teach. I wanted to wear the uniform I've always been proud of, but I thought it was time for me to do something different. I've been happy teaching for the past nine-plus years. And no matter how much you've learned here, and how all of us do everything possible to prepare you for what's ahead... the reality is this isn't reality. This is a classroom. The shooting, the fighting, the driving... it's all in a learning environment." Sean looked around the room, all eyes on him as he spoke. "The world is changing. It's harder out there than it was when I was your age. And, well... let me get right to my point." He hesitated a moment, afraid maybe his voice would crack or his emotions would get the best of him. "I've made the decision to join you on the streets."

The recruits all looked at each other and glanced around the room.

"I'm leaving my position here as an instructor at the academy and will be joining zone four. I'll be on patrol, starting with a training officer the same way each of you will be." He folded his arms and leaned back against his desk. "So, this will not only be a new beginning for all of you. But also for me."

11

DANNY SAT AT the table shaking his head. His eyes went up to the clock behind Carla. "See? This is what I mean. You can't rely on him anymore. It's two thirty... he can't even be on time?"

Veronica just stared at Carla as Curtis nodded in agreement. "He knows you're still pissed at him."

Danny made a face. "It's not even that I'm pissed. I mean, yeah, I'm pissed. But it's more about... I can't even drive my own goddamn car right now. The thing is..." He looked at everybody around the table. "We can't afford to have him involved anymore. I don't know what's going on in his brain, but he poses too much of a risk."

Veronica had her eyes down on her thick fingers, interlocked together on the table. She didn't look at Danny.

"Veronica?" he said. "Don't you agree?"

She shrugged and finally looked up. "He's our

friend. It's just, I don't know..."

"He treats you like shit. And he puts me in these spots. I mean, I never blamed him for me getting nailed, but..."

Veronica nodded and again looked down at the table. "It's not like I have men lined up to sleep with me."

Curtis laughed and looked at Veronica. "What, you don't think he'll fuck you anymore if we do this without him? Nobody's lined up for him either."

Carla put her hand on Veronica's arm. "The last thing you and I want is to spend a few years down in Marion County, just because Jimmy couldn't keep his head on straight."

Veronica looked at Carla and tilted her head. "Marion County?"

Carla picked up her vodka tonic and took a sip. She nodded and looked at Veronica over the rim. "The women's state prison, hon."

Danny got up from the table and grabbed his phone from the counter. He dialed Jimmy's number one more time. "I gotta see where the hell he is before we get ahead of ourselves."

Carla got up from her chair and walked to the window, looked down toward the parking lot. "Speak of the devil. He's outside, walking across the lot."

Curtis stood up and looked out the window. "You see his van?"

Carla didn't answer.

Veronica turned her body in the kitchen chair and looked up at Danny. "So who drives if Jimmy's not going to be in?"

He shrugged, gave Veronica a quick nod with his chin. "I thought maybe *you* could. Me and Curtis'll go in. As long as those paintings are in the same place, right there on the floor... we'll be in and out in three minutes." He turned his eyes to Curtis. "We need to strap them together, make 'em easier to carry. Might be looking at seventy-five to a hundred pounds, each of us carries six paintings."

Carla stepped toward Danny. "You make it sound so simple."

"Well," Danny said, "it's rare you have valuable paintings sitting out for anyone to take. That's why we can't screw up this opportunity. Like taking candy from an old lady." He laughed, turned to the refrigerator and pulled out a beer.

Carla said, "What makes you so sure she's not going to store them before she leaves?"

"It's possible. But let's hope she doesn't."

Carla looked over at Curtis. "You sure nobody stays there while she's gone?"

He nodded. "My understanding is the house sits empty every summer—at least for the past ten years."

There was a knock at the door. Danny sipped his beer, then put it down on the counter, reached for the chain and turned the knob.

Jimmy pushed it open and walked in past Danny without a word.

"You're an hour late," Danny said as he grabbed his beer and took another sip, looking at Jimmy over the bottle.

Jimmy was about to sit down but stopped and turned back to Danny. "What are you always up my ass for? You still pissed off about that 7-Eleven? When did you become all high and mighty... too big to hold up a store for some cash?" He shrugged. "It's not like we got caught."

Danny narrowed his eyes and took a step closer to Jimmy. "Not this time. But it's always the same shit with you. Last time, it was your little detour, got me three years in Raiford. And you didn't get shit, for what goddamn reason, I don't know. But now, I can't even drive my own car."

Jimmy's face got twisted. "Why the hell can't you drive your car?"

"Because whoever saw you come out of that 7-Eleven knows exactly what it looks like, you jackass."

Jimmy stepped in front of Danny, and the two stood chest to chest. Danny was taller with more muscle on his frame. But Jimmy was wide, even a bit dumpy with his baggy clothes hanging off him.

Danny shoved him with both hands and pushed him backward onto the table. He looked at Jimmy's clenched fist, knew he was getting ready to take a swing. "Go ahead," he said. "I dare you to throw a punch." Danny pointed to his own chin. "Right here."

Carla pulled Danny back from Jimmy.   "That's enough."

But Jimmy jumped at Danny, wrapped his arms around his neck and tried to pull him to the floor.

Danny threw his right fist up and unloaded under Jimmy's jaw. Jimmy's head whipped back, and Danny followed with a left, punched him in the back of his head. Jimmy stumbled back, but Danny grabbed him with both hands on his shoulders, held him and drove a knee into his chest. He threw Jimmy backward into the refrigerator.

Veronica screamed, "Danny, stop! You're going to kill him!"

Jimmy dropped to the floor, and Danny stood over him like a boxer after a knockout, his nostrils flared as he breathed heavy through his nose.

Veronica pushed past Danny and kneeled down next to Jimmy. Blood dripped down from his mouth.

Jimmy pushed her away from him. "Get your fat sweaty paws off of me!" He grabbed the refrigerator door's handle and pulled himself up, holding his jaw with his free hand. He stared back at Danny, his eyes narrowed.

Danny pointed toward the door. "We're done here, Jimmy. It's over."

Jimmy touched his mouth with his fingers and looked at the blood on the ends. He turned for the

door and left it wide open as he walked out into the
hallway and disappeared down the stairs.

12

NORA LEFT SEAN a message and said she was leaving a day earlier than planned. She said Gracie would be staying at her house for a while, but she didn't know for how long.

After he listened to the message, he tried to call Nora, but she didn't answer her phone at home. She carried a cell phone in her purse but she never turned it on, thought having a phone with her at all times was foolish.

By the time Sean got off work and left the academy, it was a little past six. Even though it was the evening, the sun was as bright and hot as it'd been all day.

He put down the windows in his Explorer and cranked on the AC as soon as he started the engine. Although it felt like steam coming out of the vents. He grabbed his phone and called his aunt's house one more time.

This time she answered. "Hello?"

"Aunt Nora, it's Sean. I thought I might've missed you."

"Missed me for *what*?"

"I got your message. You said you were leaving for Maine a day early. Weren't you supposed to fly up *tomorrow*?"

"Yes."

Sean sat in his car with the phone up to his ear. His elbow hung out the open window. "You left a message. I thought maybe you needed something?"

She said, "Did you listen to the whole message?"

Sean looked at his phone screen, then put it back to his ear. "I thought I did. Why?"

"I wanted to make sure you'd take care of everything on that list I gave you."

"Oh." Sean pulled open the lid on the center console and pulled out the folded piece of paper she'd given him. "You also said Gracie was staying at the house?"

"She's going to watch the place."

Sean looked over the list and wondered why she'd need him to do most of it if Gracie was going to be staying there. "I know she's your daughter, but I just think..." He stopped.

"You think *what*? What were you going to say?"

There was a moment or two of silence. "Nothing. It's fine." He was hesitant to tell Nora much about his personal business because no matter what he'd say, she'd judge him in her own way. "I'm going back on patrol. So I'll be able to keep a better eye on your house while you're away."

"Back on patrol?" He wasn't sure, but it sounded like she laughed. "Aren't you a little old?"

He should've known better. "I'm in better shape than the young recruits I'm training. I'm looking forward to it." He paused a moment. "I thought you'd be happy for me, since the last comment you made about my job was that I wasn't a real cop."

Why did he even bother?

Nora made an odd noise into the phone. "You're your own man. Do what you want."

Sean leaned his head back and put up the windows as the air-conditioner finally started to cool. "What time is your flight?"

"At six."

"It's after six."

"Six in the morning. You should pay better attention."

"But your message said..."

He heard the doorbell ring from the other end of the phone.

Nora said, "Someone's at my door. Make sure you keep an eye on the house." She hung up without another word.

Sean was on the fence about going by Nora's house

before she left. If it was just to say goodbye, he was sure it was a waste of time.

But on the other hand, he wanted to see Gracie, make sure she knew he was back on patrol and would be watching the house. The truth was, he didn't trust Gracie one bit. And he knew she must've had a reason for showing up at her mother's house after so many years. Not to mention, coming back from New York—coincidentally—a few days before the house would be empty.

He knew, if Gracie could, she'd lift the house from the foundation and sell it for scraps if it'd put a few dollars in her pocket.

He pulled up in front of her house. A cable van was parked out on the street, but he didn't pay it much attention. He continued up the driveway. Gracie's BMW wasn't there. He walked up the steps. The front door was cracked open. He pushed on it and unclipped his Glock from the holster. He stepped inside. "Aunt Nora? Gracie?"

Nobody answered.

He rested his hand on his gun but had yet to remove it. He took careful steps along the hardwood and started toward the room with the TV and the baby grand. He peeked through the doorway, being cautious. The TV was on. The volume was down.

"Aunt Nora?"

He stepped through the doorway.

Nora was on the couch with a pillow over her

head, her hands tied behind her back.

Sean hurried toward her with his gun drawn and noticed the paintings were no longer against the wall behind the baby grand. He crouched down to help her but caught a glimpse of someone coming up behind him. He turned with his gun raised. But before he could get to his feet, a man with a ski mask over his head and a thick beard coming out the bottom was on top of him.

The man swung a pipe-like object and knocked the gun from Sean's hand. The Glock slid across the hardwood.

Sean tried to get to his feet but the pipe came down again and struck him hard on the side of the head. He heard Nora's muffled scream along with the explosion he felt inside his skull when the pipe struck him again. Blood came down over his eyes. He couldn't see. He tried to get to his feet but was hit again. He stumbled into the TV and crashed down on top of it.

Sean stretched out his hands and grabbed the man's leg.

But he was hit again.

And this time, he didn't get up.

Sean opened his eyes and looked up at Gracie, kneeling over him. "Sean? Sean? Can you hear me? Sean?"

For a moment, he had no idea where he was. He tried to get to his feet, but the weight of his own head kept him down. He remembered Nora. "Where's your mother!" He pushed Gracie out of his way and tried to get to his feet one more time.

But Gracie held her hand on his chest. "She's okay. She's in the kitchen. We called nine-one-one. The rescue should be here any moment."

He put his hand to his aching head then looked at his fingers. They were covered in blood. Gracie had a towel in her hand... soaked in blood. He felt the pain everywhere. "Grace, help me up... will you?"

"Sean, you're not in good shape."

He gave her a look. "Thanks for the update." He grabbed on to her arm and pulled himself to his feet. He stumbled a bit but made his way into the kitchen. "Aunt Nora?"

Nora turned from the sink. She had a towel in her hand she ran under the faucet. She squeezed it out then walked over to Sean and gave him the soaked towel. "I told you, you were too old to be a cop."

He turned and looked back at Gracie standing behind him. "Were you here? Did you get a look at him?"

Nora shook her head. "She wasn't here. He said he was with the cable company... and I told him everything was working, that they'd already gone through the whole house. But then he pushed me back and covered my mouth with his hand. Then he covered my head with a bag and taped my hands and mouth." She shook her head. "Son of a bitch."

Sean stepped out from the kitchen and looked down behind the baby grand. "Where are the paintings?"

Nora and Gracie exchanged a look.

Gracie said, "They're gone. He took them."

There was a knock at the door. Sean held the wet towel on his head, but wasn't even sure where the blood was coming from. He walked to the front door and pulled it open. On the other side was an attractive younger woman, dressed in a uniform from the Jacksonville Sheriff's Office.

He recognized her right away and stepped back from the door. "Officer Cash?"

"Officer Coyle? I didn't realize you were..."

"This is my aunt's house... I walked in as the robbery was taking place. I got hit with a pipe, lost consciousness."

Gracie walked around the corner and greeted Officer Cash. "He did. He was out cold on the floor. My mother was tied up with her face covered. And my father's paintings were stolen."

Sean looked down at his uniform. "Shit, he took my two-way." He reached for his holster. "And my Glock." He looked at the floor where the TV screen was smashed. "Son of a bitch took my Glock."

Jenna said, "Officer Coyle, why don't you have a seat. EMTs are on their way."

13

DANNY SAT AT the far end of the counter at the Raceway gas station. The line at the cash register was longer than usual for midafternoon.

Veronica walked over to Danny and wiped her forehead with the back of her wrist. "I don't think Jimmy's coming back to work. And I don't know if they're hiring someone else or not." She grabbed a container and walked away, filled it with fried chicken and french fries and handed it to the woman on the other side of the counter. Veronica turned to Danny. "I don't get paid enough for this."

Danny watched her move as fast as she could in the tight space. She pulled hot fried chicken from the deep fryers and dumped the chicken into the metal tins under the heat lamps behind the glass. She seemed to do a good job keeping up with the rush. But the people in line grumbled.

A long-haired man dressed in a sports coat and

jeans stood in the line. He straightened his round-rim glasses and shook his head, looked like he purposely dressed the part, whatever it was. Maybe he was a so-called writer who hadn't yet written a single word. The man turned and looked at the others in line. "Can't she move that big body a little faster?" He laughed, but most of the people in line looked away or down at their phones. He looked at his watch. "Miss? Is there any way you can speed it up back there?"

Veronica turned with a container of chicken, handed it to the next woman in line behind the register and rang her up. Veronica looked at the man. "Sir? I'm moving as fast as I can."

He nodded. "Which doesn't look to be very fast, now, does it?"

Danny straightened himself on the stool, watched the man step to the register.

The man took his time, stared up at the menu on the wall and rubbed the hair on his chin. "Uhhh, I think I'll have a... no, you know what? Give me a five-piece. No dark meat. And I'd like the roasted potatoes with it. Not the greasy fries."

Veronica kept her gaze on him for a moment, then leaned over to fill the container with five pieces of chicken and the roasted potatoes. She slid it across the counter and tapped the register.

"Did you give me five pieces? I only want three."

Veronica shook her head. "Sir, you said you

wanted a five-piece."

"No, I didn't." He pulled the container toward him. "I'll keep this, but I'm only paying for three."

Danny knew Veronica was as good as anyone at keeping her cool. But she gave Danny a look, and he knew she was about to blow. But she kept her mouth shut.

The man paid with a credit card, then turned from the register and walked past Danny and toward the door. He smirked at Danny. "Large Marge must have fat between her ears too."

Danny stood and grabbed the man by the arm. "Her name's Veronica."

The man stared into Danny's eyes and ripped his arm free. He turned back to the counter. "Hey, Marge? You didn't give me my Coke."

The people standing in line stared at them.

Danny said, "You didn't order a Coke. I was right there, listening to you."

The man looked Danny up and down. "Why don't you mind your own business?"

Veronica walked over with a Coke and slid it to the man, then turned and walked away without a word. She looked at the next person in line. "Next?"

He grabbed the cup and walked past Danny and out the front door.

Danny looked back at Veronica but she'd already turned away. He walked out the door and looked around the parking lot, toward the man getting into a green Mazda convertible.

A girl's car.

He took long and hurried steps across the lot and walked up to the man about to close his door. The man had one foot still outside the door and on the ground. Danny lifted his boot and drove his heel into the side of the door, slammed it closed on the man's leg.

A crushing sound was followed by a bloodcurdling scream. The five-piece chicken and roasted potatoes flew up into the air and came back down over the man inside of the car. He looked up at Danny. He cried and screamed and tried to push open the door, but Danny hadn't yet moved his foot. "My leg! You broke my goddamn leg!"

Danny took his foot off the door, then turned and walked away. He hurried across the parking lot, past customers coming out from inside with their eyes toward the man screaming in the girl's car. He continued past the building and walked alongside an eight-foot privacy fence and into the adjacent parking lot. He stood in front of the flooring store off Dellwood Avenue. He knew he made a big mistake... the same mistake Jimmy would have made.

He'd walked a good mile before he pulled out his phone to call Carla. But he saw he'd missed a call from Veronica. He called her back.

She answered right away. "Danny?" Her voice was hushed. "The cops are here. They're asking what happened to that man outside." She paused a moment. "What did you do?"

"Keep your mouth shut, will you? I didn't do a thing. Who said I did anything?"

Veronica was quiet on the other end of the phone.

"What the hell did you tell them? I hope you didn't —"

"I didn't say a thing. You know I wouldn't. But they're asking questions. There were people out in the parking lot who saw what happened."

Danny walked along Dellwood but stayed off the road by a good twenty feet and walked from building to building.

She said, "You didn't have to do that, Danny. That guy's a real prick... comes in here all the time. I can take care of myself."

He said, "I have to go," and hung up to call Carla. She answered and Danny said, "Where are you?"

"Where am I? I'm at the apartment. Why? Where are you?"

"The corner of Dellwood and Woodruff. I need a ride. Cops are out looking for me..."

"Cops? Why? What'd you do?"

"Nothing. Just come get me. Park in the lot at a place called JT's Auto Body. I'm going to lay low until I see you."

"You gave Jimmy all that shit about putting you in

a tough spot, and here you are..."

"Jesus Christ, Carla. Just shut your fucking mouth and come get me."

14

JENNA CASH TURNED to Sean from the passenger seat of the cruiser as they headed south on Edgewood Avenue. "It must feel a little different today, not being in front of a roomful of recruits?"

He turned to her and nodded. "I know it's only been a couple of days, but I already feel like I belong out here. Like I never left." He reached above his eye, felt the ten stitches they'd put in his head from one of the hits he took at Nora's house.

Jenna kept her eyes on him. "Don't you find it strange, your aunt didn't want to talk about what happened? And then she just takes off for a vacation? You'd think she'd wait around for some answers. Or at least make sure her daughter and nephew were okay."

Sean laughed. "My aunt marches to the beat of her own drum." He glanced at Jenna. "Don't worry, she'll call me in a couple of days to make sure I get the yard taken care of."

"What about the paintings? I understand they're worth quite a bit of money, but she didn't seem concerned..."

"She doesn't care about the money. To be honest, I'm afraid she only took them so she could burn them. She never forgave my uncle. Getting her hands on those paintings was her revenge." With his eyes on the road, he said, "But you're right. They're worth money. More now that he's dead."

"Like Van Gogh," Jenna said. "I think he died broke."

Sean turned onto King Street. "The woman he left in charge of his work was his publicist. And she just happened to be his girlfriend. She's the one who put him on the map." He cracked a slight smile and gave Jenna a look. "Aunt Nora referred to her as 'the whore.'"

"Then how did she end up with the paintings?"

"Nora?" He shrugged. "She took them from the gallery. And because she and my uncle never legally divorced, she had every right to take them." He glanced at Jenna. "At least that's what she believed."

They drove quiet for a few more blocks.

Jenna said, "Is it true your cousin Gracie did time up in New York?"

Sean took a moment before he answered. "She's always been kind of a mess. Daddy's little girl... spoiled, but never got exactly what she was looking for from either parent. I'm not sure what that was, but..." He paused a moment. "My uncle left for New York to do a show. Kind of a big deal for him at the time. Nora didn't want to go. She was funny like that. I'm not sure Joseph cared whether she did or not, but he never returned to Florida. Gracie followed him, claimed Nora drove them both away."

Jenna had her eyes on Sean. "Did she?"

"Drive him away?" Sean took a moment. "You met Nora, although briefly. She doesn't exactly have what you'd call a magnetic personality. It's quite the opposite, in fact."

"Gracie lived in New York with her father?"

"No, she didn't get along with his girlfriend. I mean, I didn't exactly keep in touch with Gracie over the years, but as far as I can tell, New York didn't work out so well for her."

Dispatch came over with a suspected larceny at a Nathan's Convenience Store. The suspect was described as a bearded man driving a white van.

Jenna grabbed the radio and started to type on the computer in front of her. "Unit thirty-five responding to dispatch."

Sean flipped on the blue lights and hit a U-turn in front of St. Vincent's Medical Center at the corner of Riverside and King, crossed the yellow line and drove north.

He pulled into the parking lot outside Nathan's Convenience Store, drove past an old woman at a pump and stopped in front of the door. He jumped from the car, placed his hat on his head and followed Jenna inside the small building, packed with shelving between tight aisles, a row of glass-door coolers along the back wall.

A young girl, no more than fifteen or sixteen, stood behind the counter. Her hands shook, and tears came down her face.

"Are you the only one here?" Jenna said.

The girl nodded. "My boss is on his way now."

The bell over the door rang, and an older gentleman with shoe-polished hair and a bronze-tanned face gave Sean a nod, then asked the girl for a pack of Pall Mall cigarettes. "Everything all right, Mary Ellen?"

She nodded. "We just got robbed." She made a gun with her thumb and forefinger, pointed it at her cheek. "Man held a gun like this, right in my face. Made me empty the drawer."

"No shit?" The man glanced at Sean, turned and opened the door. The bell rang, and he walked out without another word.

Sean had his pad in his hand but had a feeling Mary Ellen didn't trust the men in blue... just by the way she looked at him. "What's your last name, Mary Ellen?"

"Shopinski."

"How do you spell that?"

"Exactly as it sounds. *Shop. In. Ski.*"

Sean looked up from his pad, gave her a look. "Why don't you go ahead and tell me exactly what happened."

"Man came in here, grabbed a six of Budweiser. Asked me for a pack of Marlboros. He turned for the door but stopped and pulled the gun from his pants, told me to empty the drawer on the counter."

"Can you tell me what he looked like?"

She paused a moment, then shrugged. "He had a beard. But I didn't take my eyes off that gun pointed my way, other than to open the damn drawer."

Sean unclipped the Glock 22 and removed it from the holster, placed it down on the counter. It was the replacement for the one he'd lost at Nora's house. "Did the gun look anything like this one?"

She looked down, then raised her eyes to Sean. "Yeah, just like that. A Glock 22."

He cracked a slight smile. "I know you didn't get a good look at him. But what about his height, compared to me?"

She looked Sean up and down. "Shorter than you. Maybe by a few inches. He stole a pair of sunglasses. Had them on when he first came up to the counter... the tag still hanging off the side. He stepped to the door just before I had a chance to ask if he was going to pay for them. That's when he turned with the Glock in his hand."

Sean looked up at the camera with duct tape wrapped around it, pointed down from behind the counter. The duct tape looked to hold it in place. "Does your camera still work?"

Mary Ellen turned and looked up behind her. "Only if someone's watchin' it from the back. Recorder don't work no more."

The bell over the door rang as Jenna walked back inside. She gave Sean a look, then shifted her eyes to Mary Ellen. "Did you get a good look at the vehicle?"

Mary Ellen nodded. "Yes, ma'am, a white van from the cable company, s'far as I could tell."

15

DANNY TURNED BACK and looked over his shoulder into the back seat. He said to Curtis, "When I said to get a car, didn't it cross your mind we'd need something bigger than a goddamn Chevy Caprice?"

Curtis glanced at Veronica out of the corner of his eye. "I thought you'd like it. It's only a couple years old."

Carla turned the wheel down Avondale Avenue, drove quiet for half a mile, then pulled the Caprice up into the driveway in front of the old two-story house. The sun had just about set and the yard was dark, other than the streetlamp shining down on the driveway. She put the car in park and turned to Danny. "Are we good?"

Danny nodded, turned back to Curtis and Veronica. "Let's go."

Veronica opened the rear passenger door first and

stepped outside. The car lifted at least six inches.

Danny turned to Curtis. "Move as fast as you can. Make sure the alarm's dead." He pushed open the passenger side door and looked over at Carla. "Be back here in five minutes. Park here, but back it in. And have the trunk open. I just hope the goddamn paintings fit." He shook his head. "Goddamn Chevy Caprice... we gotta put 'em in the back seat. Curtis can ride in the trunk." He stepped out and tossed the duffle bag over his shoulder and walked straight to the back of the house. Veronica followed behind him, and Curtis stopped off near the plastic junction box with all the wires.

The property was surrounded with thick trees and tall shrubs, enough to block any view the neighbors would've had.

Danny and Veronica stood outside the sliding glass door until Curtis came around the corner, a pair of wire cutters in his hand.

"You kill it?" Danny said.

Curtis nodded. "Her alarm's over thirty years old. I'm not sure it worked. But, yes... it's all set."

The three of them stood on the patio behind the sliding glass door and pulled their ski masks down over their faces.

Danny pulled the crowbar from his bag and slid it in the tight space between the frame of the sliding glass door. With one flip of his wrist, he cracked the frame and a long strip of wood fell to the ground.

But the door wouldn't open. He tried again and jammed the crowbar between the crack with more pressure. But the door didn't budge. "Shit, there's a lock on the door." He leaned his head against the glass and looked down at the floor on the other side of the door. "We need to use a window."

He stepped across the patio to the nearest window. He jammed the crowbar between the sash and the sill and leaned down hard with two hands. The window frame cracked, and Danny slid his fingers underneath, pushed it open. He backed away. Like a game-show host, he gestured toward the window. "Go 'head," he said to Curtis. "All yours."

"Why me?" Curtis said.

"Because you're the smallest." He pointed to Veronica with his thumb. "You expect *her* to climb through?"

Danny crouched down below the window and interlocked his fingers together to give Curtis a boost. "Climb through, then open the sliding door. The paintings are inside, behind the piano."

Curtis put his foot in Danny's hands and grabbed the inside frame of the window. He pulled himself up, and Danny pushed him from behind, sent him flying through the open window. Curtis crashed down on the other side.

Danny was up on his toes and looked in the window. "You okay?"

Curtis got up and wiped himself off. He nodded

but held his hand on the back of his head. "Shit, that hurt."

Danny stepped in front of the sliding glass door and knocked.

Curtis slid it open from the other side. He said, "Smells weird in here."

Danny walked in ahead of Veronica then sniffed in the air. "Smells like mothballs." He sniffed again. "And weed." He turned and glanced back at Veronica.

She took a sniff herself and nodded. "You're right."

Danny stood by the sliding glass door and crouched down, looked underneath the baby grand where the paintings had been. "Oh no... it can't be..." He walked around the piano and again looked down at the floor. "Holy shit." He turned to Curtis and Veronica. "She must've moved them." He looked around at the art on the walls but didn't recognize any of it. He pointed toward one of them and gave Curtis a look. "That's not one of 'em, is it?"

Curtis shook his head and leaned in closer to one of the paintings. "No, this one's by a woman."

Danny opened a closet door at the front of the house. He took the flashlight from his back pocket and shined it inside. There were shoes on the floor but nothing else. "Shit." He closed the door and scratched his head. He gave a nod toward Veronica. "Go upstairs, see if you can find the paintings." He looked down the hall and into the kitchen. "Curtis, go up and see if you can get in the attic. Maybe she put them up there."

Curtis looked at his watch. "But we don't have much time."

Danny yelled, "I said go check the fucking attic!"

Curtis followed Veronica up the stairs.

Danny yelled up. "Don't turn any lights on up there." His phone buzzed, and he pulled it from his pocket to look at the screen. It was Carla. He answered. "They're not where they were the other day. The old lady must've moved them."

Carla said, "The paintings?"

Danny didn't answer. What did she think he meant?

She said, "I knew you should've grabbed them when you were there the first time."

"Now you're a goddamn Monday morning quarterback?"

She didn't say a word back. After a brief pause, she said, "It's already been seven minutes. I'm less than a block away. What do you want me to do?"

"Give us five minutes, then pull in the driveway."

"You're the one who said Jerry Russo used to tell you more than five minutes and you double your chances of getting pinched."

Danny looked out the window. Headlights came up the driveway. "What the hell are you doing?" he said. "I told you to give us five more minutes. Go drive around the block a few times."

"Are you talking to me?" Carla said.

"Who else would I be talking to? And I told you to back the car in the driveway. And shut off the goddamn headlights... will you?"

"I'm not in the driveway. I'm in the parking lot at Edgewood Park."

Danny stepped to the side of the window and leaned against the wall. He pulled the curtain back with one finger and looked outside. The streetlight shined on what looked to be an older BMW with discolored paint and a mismatched hood. The convertible top looked to be torn. The headlights were on.

Danny turned and yelled up the stairs. "We gotta go!" He looked outside and yelled again, his voice loud but hushed. "Veronica! Curtis! Let's go. Someone's out in the driveway!"

The car's engine idled from outside.

The hardwood floor rumbled, and Veronica came down the stairs as fast as she could. Her eyes were wide and visible in the dark. She looked back and forth, her breaths heavy and labored. She looked into the light outside.

Danny pushed her from behind. "Go! Get out of here... go out back and keep moving. Call Carla, tell her to pick us up on Knight Street." He glanced toward the window, then looked up the stairs.

"Curtis! You hear me?"

Veronica hadn't moved.

"What the hell are you doing?" He snapped, "Go!"

She walked to the open sliding glass door.

Danny looked outside at the car's headlights. Nobody had stepped out of the car. He turned back and looked up the stairs. "Curtis? Where the hell are you?" He glanced out through the window one more time then ran up the stairs. "Curtis!"

The wooden ladder extended down from the attic at the top of the stairs. Danny lifted the ski mask up off his face and stood at the foot of the ladder and looked up through the hole. He saw the light from Curtis's flashlight as it bounced around the rafters. "Curtis!" he yelled again, louder this time, but still with a hush to his voice.

Danny heard steps above his head, from down the other end of the hall. He followed the sounds with his eyes.

Curtis's foot smashed through the ceiling. Dust glowed in the light from the lamp outside as chunks of drywall fell to the floor.

"Holy shit!" Danny said. He looked up along the ceiling and ran down the hall.

A leg stuck out through the plaster.

"I'm stuck!" Curtis yelled, his voice muffled above the ceiling.

Danny's heart pumped hard in his chest. He looked down at the bottom of the stairs. He was sure the front door was about to open, and they would be caught inside Nora's house. He reached around his back and felt for the .38 Special in his waistband. He didn't remove it but made sure it was there. "Kill or be killed," was the voice he heard in his head. It was Jerry Russo, and the words he said when he first gave Danny the gun.

Jerry himself had only killed one man. Or so he said.

Danny reached up for the sneaker above his head, then wrapped his arms around Curtis's legs and squeezed. Without a word he stood up tall on his toes then used the force of his own body to yank Curtis out from the ceiling.

Curtis crashed down on top of Danny. They hit the floor. Dust and drywall and pieces of fiberglass insulation covered them both.

Danny threw Curtis off of him then stopped in his tracks.

A key slipped into the lock at the front door. He reached down and helped Curtis to his feet.

They both watched the stairs.

Curtis whispered. "What are we going to do?"

Danny rolled the ski mask down over his face and reached back, removed the .38 Special from his pants and gave Curtis a look. "Kill or be killed."

Curtis shook his head. "Are you serious?" He looked down at the gun in Danny's hand. "We hit this place because there wasn't supposed to be anyone home. Come on, man. You can't—"

The door at the bottom of the stairs opened. Danny looked down from the darkness as an attractive woman walked through the door. He stepped back behind the wall and gave Curtis a look. Danny knew just a few more steps and she'd see the open back door with the broken frame... the open window... the open closet door.

He gave Curtis one nod and ran down the stairs.

The light came on and the woman screamed.

Danny took the corner from the stairs and pointed his .38 at her head. She didn't move. And she didn't scream. She stared past his gun and looked into his eyes behind the ski mask. She looked over her shoulder, then ran toward the open sliding glass door and straight out into the yard.

Danny held the gun and pointed it at her back, but he couldn't bring himself to pull the trigger. He ran after her. "Stop!" he yelled. "Don't make me shoot you!"

She was halfway across the yard and headed for the tall live oaks along the back.

Danny tucked his .38 in his waistband. He had both hands stretched out, grabbed her by the back of her shirt and pulled her down to the ground.

She let out a scream, and he turned her on her back, straddled her and put his open hand over her mouth.

She kicked and twisted back and forth and took a

bite of his hand then lifted her knee, caught him square in the balls.

Danny reached for his crotch, and she threw him from her, jumped to her feet and started to run. But he grabbed her by the foot just as she took a step and held on tight with both hands.

She fell back to the ground and took one wild swing after another, landed a couple of shots on Danny's face.

Curtis came out of nowhere and knocked her away from Danny. She threw another wild punch, hit Curtis in the ear.

But Danny pulled out his .38 and stuck it in her face, had it pressed above her eye. "Throw another punch... I'll pull the goddamn trigger."

Curtis got up and tried to help her from the ground, but she stood up and shoved him one more time.

Danny pulled the hammer back on his .38. "Don't make me shoot you."

She turned to Danny. "Get that gun out of my face."

Danny gave Curtis a look and laughed, then each grabbed one of her arms and walked her across the lawn toward the house.

"What's your name?" Danny said.

She didn't answer right away.

"Gracie."

He said, "What are you doing in the old lady's

house?"

She gave him a look. "It's my house. The *old lady* is my mother."

Danny's eyes were on Curtis, but neither said a word.

"What do you want with me?" Gracie said.

They stepped through the open sliding glass door and into the house. Danny scratched the top of his head. The sweat under the itchy mask made it uncomfortable. He remembered Jerry Russo preferred nylon stockings. "You can breathe," he'd say. Danny gave Curtis a nod. "Grab the duct tape from my bag."

Curtis crouched down and reached into the duffle bag Danny'd left in the middle of the room. He held up a roll of duct tape.

Danny held Gracie's arms with both hands. "Wrap her wrists. Then tear off a piece, put it over her mouth." Danny whispered into Gracie's ear. "Sorry. Just until we figure out what the hell we're going to do here."

Gracie shook her head. "No, please. Don't. Come on, you don't have to——"

Curtis slipped the tape over her mouth, tore off another bigger piece and did it again, just in case.

16

SEAN HAD THE day off and met Mac for breakfast at the Silver Car Diner, a fifties-themed restaurant off St. Johns Bluff Road, not far from the convenience store that'd been robbed two days earlier.

Sean said, "Then we get a call, a man was assaulted outside that same Raceway..."

"On Cassat?"

"Same one we went to. Man was assaulted by another man in the parking lot. Had his leg snapped in his car door... fried chicken and a soda dumped all over the place."

Mac made a face. "Car was stolen?"

Sean shook his head and ripped a piece from his bagel and stuck it in his mouth. "Victim said he saw the same man at the counter but swore he hadn't spoken a word to him. I'm not sure I believe him, but..."

Mac laughed. "So there's more action in Riverside than you expected, huh?"

Sean huffed out a slight laugh. "Veronica Hobson was behind the counter again. But she said she didn't see a thing, the place was too busy. Also said she didn't know the man at the counter, but another witness said she saw her talking to him." Sean sipped his orange juice. "Went back to talk to her, turns out she doesn't work there anymore. Manager didn't make it clear why. Unrelated to the incident, from what she said."

Mac just stared back at Sean, shoved half a muffin in his mouth.

Sean's phone rang, and he looked down at the screen. He put his finger up toward Mac. "Give me a second." Sean answered the phone. "Sean Coyle."

"Hello, sir, this is Renzo. The landscaper at your aunt's house. We're over here now, cutting the lawn, and the back door's wide open."

"Isn't someone there? Nora's daughter should be inside." He looked at his watch. "Assuming she's awake."

"No, sir. I stuck my head in there, but nobody answered when I called. There's a window open, too... looks like it's busted. The wood part. The frame on the door looks broken, too. I think the house has been broken into."

Sean jumped up from the chair. "I'll be right there." He slipped his phone back in his pocket, picked up his juice, and threw back what was left in the cup.

Mac looked up at Sean. "What's wrong?"

Sean pulled a couple of bills from his wallet and tossed them on the table. "The landscaper thinks Nora's house has been broken into."

"Again?"

Sean shook his head. "Gracie's in the house for a week and already... this shit happens. Sorry to cut it short. We'll have to do this another time." He gave Mac a nod. "I hope retirement's doing you all right..." Sean pulled out his phone and started for the door. He dialed Gracie's number and walked outside.

But all he got was Gracie's voicemail and hung up. He stepped into the Explorer and took off right away, pulled out onto St. Johns Bluff Road and tried Gracie again. He left a message. "Gracie, it's Sean. I'm on my way to your mother's house. Not sure where you are, but..." He hesitated a moment. "The lawn guy just called me... said the back door's wide open." He passed a couple of cars on the right and picked up speed. "Call me back as soon as you get this, let me know you're okay."

Sure enough, when Sean showed up at his aunt's house, four sheriff's vehicles were parked out on the road. One parked behind Gracie's BMW.

Officer Jenna Cash was already there and stood in the hallway at the top of the stairs.

Sean headed up and followed her eyes up toward the hole in the ceiling. He looked down at the floor and the white powder-like debris and insulation and broken chunks of plaster that had fallen from the ceiling.

Jenna said, "Connor and Jackson are out back. There are tracks through the grass. It's torn up... looks like something went down back there. Just not sure what it is."

Sean looked down at the bottom of the stairs. "You didn't have to come over here on your day off. But I appreciate it."

She gave him a nod, then shifted her eyes back in the direction of the ceiling.

Sean walked down the stairs and stood at the front door. He looked out at Gracie's BMW. Jenna walked down the stairs, and he turned to her from the door. "I can't help wonder if Gracie had something to do with this."

Jenna walked past him and out the door. She stood on the top step with her back to him, her eyes out on the road.

Sean walked past her and took the walkway to the back of the house.

Jenna followed behind him. "Did you call your aunt yet?"

He looked down at his phone in his hand. "I was

hoping I'd hear from Gracie before I did. I'll call her."

Jenna grabbed Sean's arm and looked him in the eye. "Sean, she needs to know her daughter's missing."

He stopped and turned to her. "Gracie's not missing. Not yet."

They both continued to the back. Sean stopped and looked down at the splintered wood on the patio, just outside the sliding glass door.

"I think you should call Nora," she said. "Unless you want me to?"

He laughed. "You don't want to do that. It's hard enough talking to her when there's good news to share." He tapped the screen of his phone.

Nora answered on the first ring. "Hello?"

"Aunt Nora, it's Sean. How are things up there?"

"Why are you calling me this early?"

He looked at his watch. "It's almost eleven."

"Well, I'm having breakfast."

He paused a moment. "I have something I need to tell you."

She sighed into the phone. "Well, hurry up, before my eggs get cold."

Sean gave Jenna a look, wished for a moment he'd just let her make the call. "Your house has been broken into."

"That's what you're calling me about? Did that hit on your head affect your memory? I was the one tied up. Maybe you should see a doctor, if..."

"Nora, your house was broken into last night. Or sometime between yesterday and this morning."

Nora was quiet on the other end.

"Aunt Nora?"

"Was it the same person?"

"I don't know just yet, we're—"

"What do you mean you don't know? Aren't you the one keeping an eye on my house?"

Sean glanced at Jenna watching him on the phone. He said, "We're investigating. But there's more..."

"Oh no," she said. "What did they take?"

17

CARLA STOOD OVER the stove with a spatula in her hand. Blue flames shot out from under the cast-iron pan, and she turned to Danny as she flipped a grilled cheese over. "After we feed her, you have to figure out what to do with her." She shook her head. "We're not kidnappers."

Danny sipped his Jim Beam. "She has to know where the old lady hid the paintings." He nodded at Carla. "Bring her that food, see if she's ready to talk."

Carla turned the knob on the stove and flipped the grilled cheese onto a plate. "It's been two hours, she hasn't said a word. I'm afraid it's going to take more than a grilled cheese."

Veronica stood quiet, her arms folded across her big chest. She licked her lips, her eyes on the grilled cheese. She reached out for the plate and took it from Carla's hand. "Let me bring it to her. I'll see if she'll talk to me."

Curtis stood from the table with a ski mask in his hand. "But put this on."

Danny gave Veronica a nod. "If you can get her to tell us where those paintings are, then go right ahead." He reached across the table and took the ski mask from Curtis, tossed it over to Veronica but it landed on top of the grilled cheese.

Carla said, "I don't think she can see us with two pillow cases over her head."

Danny shrugged. "Play it safe."

Carla laughed as she took the plate back from Veronica. "Come on, hon. We'll both go in there... have a lady's chat." She smiled, and the two started down the hall.

Veronica stopped. "Shouldn't we bring her a drink?"

Danny reached up into the cabinet for a glass, ran it under the faucet, and handed it to Veronica. "Here."

She took it from his hand and stared back at him for a moment. "From the tap?"

Danny rolled his eyes. "Just give her the goddamn water." He sat back down at the table and watched Veronica turn her body through the doorway and follow Carla. "And put on the masks," he said. He looked up at Curtis. "Will you sit down? You're making me nervous." Danny shifted his eyes to the table. His knee bounced up and down. He tapped his fingers on top.

Curtis pulled out a chair and sat across from Danny. "What now?"

"What *now*?" Danny stared back at him. "You tell *me*. You're the one who turned us on to this gig. And now we might end up shit out of luck."

"It's not my fault," Curtis said. "But maybe Carla was right. We should've taken it when we had the chance... when we first went to the old lady's house?"

Danny narrowed his eyes and leaned forward on the table. He pointed his finger at Curtis's face. "Don't give me any shit. Coulda, shoulda... goddamn Monday morning quarterback." He leaned back in his chair. "Why don't you just put that big brain of yours to work?"

Curtis didn't respond right away. He leaned closer to Danny. "What if we use her as ransom? Get the old lady to pay for her safe return?"

Danny shook his head. "That's not my bag. I don't want to be involved in kidnapping and all the shit that goes along with it."

Curtis laughed. "You forget you have someone in the bedroom back there? What do you call that? A houseguest?"

Danny tossed back what was left in his glass and wrapped his hand around the neck of the empty bottle. He gripped it hard, and his face got tight, like he was about to flip the bottle down, smash it on the table. But he eased up his grasp and turned his eyes toward the bedroom down the hall. "They better be gettin' her to talk."

The bedroom door opened. Carla walked out ahead of Veronica with a look on her face Danny wasn't sure he liked.

He followed her with his eyes until she was next to the table. He stood up and folded his arms over his chest. "What happened?"

Carla's look turned to a smile. She glanced over her shoulder at Veronica. "She was right. Veronica got her to talk."

Danny waited. "What'd she say?"

Carla dropped the smile from her face. "You're not going to like it." She took a moment, then nodded with her eyes on the chair behind Danny. "You might want to sit down."

He shook his head. "Just tell me what she said, will you?"

"Someone else broke into the house while the old lady was home. The paintings were stolen."

Danny stared back at her but kept quiet for a moment. He ran his hand through his thick hair and closed his eyes. His breathing grew heavy. He turned and picked up the wooden chair behind him and smashed it down on the floor, startled everyone and they all exchanged a look.

"You want the rest?" Carla said, her eyes down on the broken chair. "She said he wore a mask, but he had a long, thick beard. She doesn't know anything else because she wasn't actually home at the time. Her mother was."

Danny stared into Carla's eyes and took a moment before he said what he was thinking. "You telling me Jimmy took those paintings?"

Carla nodded. "Sounds like him. He also knocked out her cousin, who surprised him while he was taking the paintings... tied up the old lady." She paused a moment. "Her cousin's a cop, with the sheriff's office."

Danny walked across the kitchen and leaned with his hands on the counter, arms wide apart. He stared at the wall, took a few deep breaths and shook his head. "Fucking Jimmy. I should've known he'd do something like this. That goddamn piece of shit..."

Veronica finally opened her mouth. "But he didn't take all the paintings."

Everyone turned to Veronica.

She nodded. "Yeah, as I was leaving the bedroom she said the paintings he took weren't worth as much as the others."

Danny said, "What others?"

"She said there are others. I asked her where they were... she just took a bite of her grilled cheese and stared back at me."

Danny stared back at Carla. "She wouldn't tell you?"

Carla shook her head. "She said the paintings aren't worth as much as everyone thinks."

Curtis stepped over the broken chair. "How do you know she's telling the truth?"

They all stood quiet for a moment.

Carla said, "So what are we supposed to do with her? Especially considering her cousin's a cop..."

Veronica said, "My dad was chief of police. If I'd gone missing he probably would've called off the search."

Danny rolled his eyes. "We *all* have mommy and daddy issues." He looked at Carla. "Do me a favor, go back in there and get her to talk. I want to know what she knows. And how much those paintings are worth..."

Carla looked down the hall toward the bedroom then shook her head. "You need to be patient, Danny. Let's just give her a little time. Once she realizes we're not going to hurt her, maybe she'll tell us what we need to know."

Danny gave Carla a look. "Who said we weren't going to hurt her?"

18

ONE OF THE detectives came out the front door of Nora's and signaled for Sean. The detective had a clear plastic bag with a pot pipe inside. He held open the bag and stuck it under Sean's nose. "Your aunt smokes marijuana?"

Sean pushed the bag away from his face. "Where'd you find it?"

"Upstairs. In one of the bedrooms."

Sean shrugged with a slight smile. "Maybe it's my aunt's."

The detective had a blank stare for a moment, unsure, then turned and walked back into the house.

Jenna said, "You don't really think Gracie's involved in what happened, do you?"

Sean looked off at the street for a moment before he answered. "I just can't get past the fact she shows up here out of the blue... knows my aunt's getting ready to leave for the summer." He looked back toward the house. "Maybe someone else sent her. I know she didn't get along with my uncle's mistress, but..."

"Just so I understand, your uncle never divorced your aunt because he didn't want to give her half of what he owned? Are you sure that's true?"

Sean gave her a look, then turned and walked inside the house. She followed behind him, and he looked at her over his shoulder. "I'm going by what Nora'd always said. But it's not like we ever had a deep and personal conversation, either."

"What about the rest of your family?"

He stopped at the door. "What about? My father's dead. My mother and I don't talk much anymore... and nobody at all ever talks to Nora."

"Just you and Gracie?"

Sean squinted his eyes. "What's this got to do with?"

"I don't know. Thought maybe family might have —"

"*Family* has nothing to do with this."

"I mean, with Gracie. Maybe someone knows something. Or are you supposed to pretend she's not related?"

Sean was at the sliding glass door and looked back at the piano. "I'm going to do my job the way I'm supposed to." He slid open the glass door and walked across the patio. He stopped where the tracks started through the grass. He looked toward the small part of the yard that'd been cut until the landscaper stopped once he noticed something wrong.

He crouched down and ran his eyes from the patio to the circle where the lawn was matted down. He looked in the direction of the trees and shrubs along the back of Nora's property, thick enough you couldn't see much of the neighbor's house at all.

He was happy there wasn't any blood. Part of him wished Gracie was somehow involved and not a victim of a crime. He'd rather be mad than worried.

He straightened out and walked through the shrubs and ended up at a fence along the back of the neighbor's backyard. He walked until he made his way through an opening, stepped across the neighbor's yard and continued through the front until he hit Knight Street. He stopped and looked back and forth along the sidewalk.

It was quiet, except for a handful of cars on the street and the swooshing sound of an irrigation system feeding the green lawn on the other side of the street. He looked back at the two-story house behind him, with a covered landing at the top of the stairs. He walked to the front door and looked up at a camera mounted under the peak of the roof over the stairs.

He turned to look when he heard a car behind him on the street.

Jenna had the passenger window down and looked

out toward him from the driver's seat. "What are you doing?"

Sean walked up to her and looked back over his shoulder at the house. "There's a camera back there, just over the door. I'm wondering what it might've caught. Thought it might be worth it if we took a look. Whoever came out the back of Nora's yard ended up out here on this street. Probably had a car waiting."

"Well, they're looking at the front of Nora's house now. Detectives believe the car was parked out on Avondale."

"They might've been dropped off. But it doesn't mean they left the same way. Especially if something went down outside behind Nora's... might've had to make a run out of there."

Jenna looked at the house. "Good chance a camera's not going to pick much up out here at night. Not when it's dark."

Sean gave her a look. "Wouldn't hurt to take a look."

Jenna put the car in park and stepped out, walked around the front and followed Sean up the walkway.

He walked up the stairs ahead of her and rang the doorbell.

A middle-aged man with gray short hair and round metal glasses opened the door. He gave Sean a nod. "I saw you both out here, wondered if you were coming to get me." He smiled and held his hands up, out in front of his shoulders. "Whatever it is... I didn't do it."

Sean didn't crack a smile, turned over his shoulder then back to the man. "This is Officer Jenna Cash. I'm Officer Sean Doyle."

The man had his eyes on Jenna. "You related to Johnny?"

Sean and Jenna both exchanged a look, but neither answered.

Sean said, "May I ask you your name, sir?"

"Ted. Ted Francis."

Sean stepped down the stairs and looked up at the camera, just below the roof. "Ted, does this camera still work?"

Ted nodded. "Oh, yes. Of course. It's pretty neat... motion activated. I can keep an eye on things outside. Mostly, I just see wildlife, opossums... squirrels." He held up his phone. "I was watching the two of you out there on the street before you came to the door." Ted handed him the phone. "See?"

Sean looked down at the screen then turned toward the street. "You get a pretty good view?" He handed the phone back to Ted.

Ted nodded. "I wanted to make sure I got the right angle. You never know. Sometimes we have our cars parked out front, or we have guests. This way, we can at least keep an eye on things."

Sean said, "So any motion on the street will

activate the camera?"

"For the most part. It's not perfect, but for a couple hundred dollars..."

Jenna said, "You store all the footage on your phone?"

Ted shook his head. "It's in the cloud."

Sean had his back to Ted, stared out at the cruiser. "Do you delete the footage?"

"I keep meaning to clean it out, but I have plenty of storage space."

Sean turned back, put his foot up on the bottom step. "You mind if we take a look at the footage from the last couple of nights?"

Ted shook his head. "Not at all." He looked down at his phone. "I have a conference call in five minutes. But if you give me your email address, I can send you access to everything on here." He smiled. "I have nothing to hide."

<h1 style="text-align:center">19</h1>

DANNY CALLED JIMMY and left him another message, said to call him back... that he just wanted to talk. He slammed the phone down on the table. "He's probably three hundred miles away from here by now."

Carla put her hand on Danny's back. "We don't even know which ones he took." She looked down the hall. "And I'm not sure she does, either."

Danny said, "Jimmy'll flip them for pennies on the dollar, think he made out on the deal."

Veronica made a face and shook her head. "We don't even know for sure it was Jimmy who took them."

Danny gave her a look, glanced at Carla and Curtis, and shook his head. He stepped to the window and stood quiet, his eyes out on the street. "Trust me, it was Jimmy. And it's just like him. He'd do it for spite... know he'd cut my legs off going in there, taking *my* goddamn paintings." He turned from the window.

Carla leaned back against the counter. "Maybe we should focus on trying to find the other paintings?"

Curtis said, "We can't go back to the house. If the cops aren't crawling around, the cousin will have his eye on the place."

Danny turned and sat at the table, his elbows down and his hands folded together in front of his chin. "I imagine the old lady'll be coming back from her trip, no? Your place gets broken into and your daughter's missing... don't you cut your vacation short?"

Curtis sat down across from Danny. "What if we wait a few days, go in when the old lady's there? Maybe we grab her, throw her in the trunk and scare her a bit until she talks..."

Veronica shook her head. "Would you want someone throwing *your* mother in the trunk?"

Danny got up from his seat, turned and lifted the shirt off his back. "See these scars? All I can say is my mother's lucky cancer got her before I was old enough to know she was the devil's daughter."

Carla took a few steps toward the hallway, then turned back to everyone else. "I'll go talk to her again. But she clearly doesn't give a shit. She spent a couple years in prison, you know. In Upstate New York."

Danny shrugged and stared back at Carla. "What's

that got to do with anything?"

Carla held her gaze on him for a moment but didn't respond.

Danny looked around the kitchen. "Carla's ex already has a buyer lined up for us in Italy. So if we don't find those paintings..."

"France," she said. "But if Charles finds out this involves a kidnapping, he's not going to want anything to do with it."

Danny got up and walked to the refrigerator, pulled out a can of beer and cracked it open. He leaned back against the counter, tipped his head back, and emptied the can of beer down his throat.

Curtis got up from the table and glanced down the hall. "Maybe we need to take care of her first, then worry about Jimmy."

Danny shook the empty can, took one last sip, and tossed it in the sink. "What, you want to kill her?"

Curtis shook his head. "No, of course not. But you think you're just going to let her go free?"

Veronica had been quiet but finally spoke up. "If she hasn't seen any of our faces, why *can't* we just let her go?"

Danny laughed. He stared back at Veronica. "Are you serious? You don't think she's got enough on us at this point? She'll lead her cousin right back here."

"I agree with Veronica," Carla said. "Her eyes have been covered. And we wore masks when we went in the room. At least if we let her go, it'll keep the sheriff's office from looking for her."

"You think they'll stop looking for us? Just because we let her go?" He ran his hand through his hair and looked around the kitchen. "Where are the keys to the Caprice?"

Carla said, "I don't think it's safe to drive that around right now."

Danny closed his eyes for a brief moment, took a breath. "Just tell me where you put the goddamn keys, Carla. I just want to drive by the old lady's house... see what the story is. I can't imagine the cops are still there."

Carla stepped across the kitchen and reached into a bowl filled with mail. She pulled out a set of keys and stuck them in her pocket.

Danny reached out his hand, his palm facing up. "Give me those keys."

Carla glanced over at Curtis. "Can you get us another car?"

"Well, they're not free," Curtis said. "And I don't know about you, but I don't have money for another one."

Carla looked down at the keys in her hand then dangled them out toward Danny. He ripped them from her hand, grabbed another beer from the fridge, and pulled open the door. "I'll be back." He turned before he closed the door and gave Veronica a nod. "See what else you can get out of her."

Danny didn't drive by Nora's house and had no intention of doing so. He instead jumped on 295, headed south, and crossed the St. Johns on the Buckman Bridge toward 95. He turned onto Southside Boulevard and pulled the Caprice into a parking lot, looked up at the apartment building where Jimmy had been living.

Jimmy moved out to where rent was cheap, but it was too far from Carla's apartment. So Danny hadn't even been by since Jimmy first moved in.

He stepped from his car and walked across the lot, looked up toward the second-floor windows and took the stairs. They were garden-style apartments, the floor outside each apartment made of wood decking material.

He stopped at the second floor and looked at all the doors. He couldn't remember exactly which apartment was Jimmy's but turned to Apartment 207. He was pretty sure that was it and leaned his ear against the door. He listened inside, but all he could hear was his own heart beating. He was furious Jimmy took those paintings right out from under his nose, like taking money out of his pocket.

Danny knocked. But after a few minutes he turned from the door. He started down the stairs, thought he'd grab a pry bar from his bag in the trunk.

But he stopped after one step, looked out and spotted a sheriff's vehicle driving slow between the cars in the lot... not far at all from where he'd parked the Caprice.

He turned and looked back up the stairs, thought maybe he should stay up on the second floor... maybe wait it out. He went halfway up the stairs but stopped. He turned and looked out into the lot.

The sheriff's vehicle was stopped behind the Caprice.

Danny continued up and walked across the decking to the back of the building. He leaned on the railing and looked down at a pond at the bottom of a steep hill. It was a long jump, but he wondered if he could make it if he had to. But he had no idea why the cops were there. Could've been for Jimmy. Or maybe they saw the Caprice. Carla was right. Although they could've been there for anything, maybe had nothing to do with Danny at all.

No need to panic, he thought.

He heard a voice from behind him, down from the front stairs. A male's voice. Then the other, a female. He knew right then he couldn't hang around to find out why they were there.

He leaned on the railing and looked down toward the ground. If the pond was closer he could jump straight in. But it wasn't. He couldn't think about it. He just had to do it. The voices were moving closer.

He looked back one more time, then without another thought, he tossed himself over the side.

He crashed hard onto the ground and rolled down

the hill until he hit the edge of the pond. There was quite a bit of pain in his wrist from how he'd landed. It wasn't a long jump, but it hurt when he hit the damp grass. He held his wrist and stood up. He looked up at the second floor then ran as fast as he could into the woods.

20

SEAN TURNED FROM the pond and looked up toward the railing on the second floor of the apartment building. "That's a good jump from up there." He turned back to Jenna. "You're sure you saw someone jump?"

Jenna gave him a look. "Of course I'm sure. He had long hair and a green shirt."

The manager of the building was a middle-aged woman, somewhere between forty and sixty with grayish hair and a cigarette in her hand. She stood under the overhang of the building on the ground floor and dangled a pair of keys. "I'll open the door if you want to go inside. Cleaning crew's supposed to be here this afternoon."

Sean and Jenna followed the woman up the stairs.

She slipped the key into the lock of Jimmy's apartment and pushed open the door, then turned to Sean and Jenna. "So what'd he do?"

Sean tried to look into the apartment. "That's what we're here to find out." He stepped past her, and the odor inside the place hit him hard. It was a strange smell, although not unexpected with a garbage can full of trash and the floor covered with papers and food containers and empty cans of Pabst Blue Ribbon. Otherwise, the place was empty.

The manager stood in the doorway and looked around. "He told us he was leaving. But at first he said it'd be another month. And he promised he'd pay what was due. So we gave him some extra time."

Sean stepped over the cans on the floor and looked back. "You always do that? Give tenants more time if they're late on their rent?"

She shook her head. "There are laws. But he'd seem to always come up with cash when he needed it." She shrugged and pulled a cigarette from the pack in her shirt pocket, stuck it in her mouth but didn't light it. "I would always cut him some slack. But once the eviction process starts..." She walked toward Sean and stopped, stuck her head through a doorway and into the bedroom. "He was pretty mad. Came in the office, kicked over a couple chairs. We almost called the sheriff's office, but..."

"That was yesterday?" Sean said.

She nodded. "We saw him move out. Didn't have much. Stuck it all in the back of his van and that was it." She looked down at the floor. "He could've at least cleaned the place."

"A white van?" Jenna said.

The woman nodded. "He worked for the cable company. Although someone else thought he worked at Raceway, out there across the river where they sell that fried chicken... off Cassat Avenue?"

Sean looked at the stained walls. More than a few fist-sized holes had been busted through. He cracked a slight smile and looked at Jenna. "Guess he loses his security deposit?"

The woman laughed. "It's the people who don't have any money... they'll leave the place a mess anyway. Even if it means losing their deposit."

Sean crouched down and picked up an empty Pabst Blue Ribbon can. "Bet these came from Nathan's Convenience."

Jenna pulled open the closet door, looked up and down, but it was mostly empty.

Sean turned to the woman. "You might want to open up some windows in here."

Jenna turned from the closet and held up a plastic name tag with *Jimmy* printed on it.

"Nothing else?" he said as he turned back to the woman. "Have you ever seen him around with anybody else? Friends? Or anyone you might be able to describe?"

She tilted her head and looked up at the dirty ceiling, her eyes squinted as if she was trying to think. She shrugged. "He was usually alone. Although we don't bother the tenants much, unless they come in the office." She turned from the doorway. "Speaking of the office, I have to get back. You're welcome to look around. Just bring me the key once you're done."

Jenna had a clear plastic baggie in her hand filled with the name tag and a few other items she picked up off the floor. She pulled off her rubber gloves. "I think we're all set if you'd like to lock up yourself."

Sean headed for the door. "If you wouldn't mind, could you hold off on having the cleaning crew come in for one more day? It's not a crime scene or anything, but..."

The woman nodded and walked out of the apartment.

Sean and Jenna drove north on 115 on their way to 90. His foot was heavy on the gas, passing cars but with the lights off.

He turned to Jenna in the passenger seat. "You mind checking with Riley, see if he's had a chance to look over that footage? I'd be interested to hear whether or not a white cable van'll show up on it leaving my aunt's house."

Jenna nodded as she pulled out her phone and tapped the screen. She put her finger up to Sean. "Riley, hey, it's Jenna. Just checking to see if anyone's looked at that footage yet, from the home on Knight Street?" She was quiet as Sean turned off 115 onto

Gate Parkway, headed east toward the St. Johns Town Center. "A Caprice?"

Sean turned and gave her a look.

She said, "What color? What about inside? Were you able to make out any faces?" Her eyes were on Sean as she listened to Riley on the other end. "Not even the driver?" She exchanged a look with Sean and shook her head, then tapped the screen and put the phone down on her lap.

Sean turned to her, anxious to hear what Riley had said. "Well?"

"They're still going through the footage, trying to improve the resolution. But, so far they can't even get the plate. The car was moving fast when they drove past the man's house. And he said the camera was too far from the road."

"Come on. They don't have anyone who can clean up the footage? At least get a face?"

"Well, for now we know it's a maroon Chevy Caprice. Two- or three-year-old model."

Sean turned the wheel and pulled into the St. Johns Town Center. He gave Jenna a quick look. "Nothing about a van?"

Jenna held her eyes on Sean and didn't answer. He could see in her face her wheels were turning. "We have to go back to Jimmy's apartment. I saw a maroon car parked outside. I'm almost certain it was a Caprice."

21

DANNY HELD HIS wrist and stared straight ahead at the TV behind the bar. He picked up his Jim Beam with his good hand and didn't turn when Carla walked up behind him.

She ran her hand across his neck and down his back, sat down on the stool next to him and stared. "You okay?"

He held his glass up to his mouth, his eyes on the TV. "Where the hell've you been?"

"Where have I been?" She raised her hand for the bartender and ordered a Captain Morgan and Coke. "You said you were going to the old lady's house. But here you are on the other side of the river." She grabbed her drink from the bartender before it even hit the bar. She turned in her stool to Danny and took a sip. "I know you came out here looking for Jimmy."

He looked at the clock up on the wall and turned,

132

finally gave her a look. "You got any cash?"

She stared back at him without an answer, snorted out her nose and shook her head.

Danny said, "I need those paintings. And I'm going to find Jimmy and get them." He sipped his Jim Beam. "Like Jerry always used to say, 'Set your eyes on the prize... then you go get it.'"

Carla took another sip of her Captain and Coke and straightened out in her stool. She placed the glass down on top of the bar. "Maybe there comes a time you have to face the fact some things aren't attainable, sweetie." She picked up her glass and took another sip.

He stared at her, his elbows up on the bar and his chin pressed into his shoulder. "I hate when you act like that," he said. "You're my girlfriend, not my mother." He kept his eyes on her as she held her drink up in front of her. Sometimes he really felt the age difference between them.

She turned again to face him, pressed her knees up against his thigh. "I spoke to Charles," she said.

"Fuck. Really? He knows I don't have the paintings?"

She nodded as she took another sip, her eyes on Danny from over the glass.

"What'd he say?"

She didn't answer him.

Danny put down his drink and grabbed her wrist. He had his lips pulled back tight on his teeth. "Carla?

Tell me what he said!"

She looked down into her glass and paused, took a moment before she said a word. "You really want to know?"

He stared back at her and nodded.

"He said you're an amateur, and if it wasn't for me you'd have to pay him for the trouble he went through to line up the buyer."

Danny slapped his free hand down on the bar then winced and grabbed his wrist. "Shit." He ran his hand through his long hair and turned away. He shook his head. "Fuck, Carla. Why'd you tell him it fell through? I'm not done yet. And I'm going to get those goddamn paintings."

"But Jimmy didn't take the ones worth all the money."

Danny made a face. "We don't know that."

"You think the girl lied? For what?" She finished what was in her glass and waved for the bartender. When he looked, she pointed to both of their glasses. She said to Danny, "Whether Jimmy has the right ones or not, you think he'd just wait around his apartment for you to show up?" She kept her eyes on him but he stared straight ahead. She turned and looked toward the door. "Where's the Caprice?"

Danny was hunched over the bar. He rubbed his wrist, moved his hand with his fingers stretched straight out, and tried to make the pain go away.

The bartender put two drinks down on the bar.

Carla said, "Put it on my tab, hon." She looked down at Danny's wrist. "You hurt your hand when you fell?"

He shook his head. "Who said I fell? I jumped."

She reached for his hand. "Let me look."

She barely touched it and he pulled it back. "That hurts!"

"Jesus," she said. "You sure it's not broken?" She put her hand behind him and rubbed his back, then slid it down and tucked her fingers into the back of his pants.

He straightened out in his seat. "What the hell are you doing?"

Carla looked at Danny and bit her lower lip once he turned to her. She moved her hand along his leg. "You're so tense." She shrugged, put on the shy-girl act. "Maybe you need to release a little tension."

Danny raised his eyebrows and tossed the shot of Jim Beam down his throat.

Carla looked around the bar, made sure nobody paid them much attention, then moved her hand around to the front of Danny's pants. She slid it between his thighs. With her free hand she finished half her drink and put down the glass. She waved to the bartender. "I'll take that tab now, sweetie."

Carla and Danny walked side by side down Baymeadow Road. She leaned into him, grabbed his good hand and gave it a squeeze.

But his eyes went up ahead, on his Buick LeSabre. He pulled his hand from hers. "You drove my Buick?" He shook his head, looked around. "I told you we can't have that out on the road. Who knows if the cops are..."

"Curtis got you a new plate. Same make and model. Got a friend of his to replace the window. I thought you'd be happy."

He pulled his hand from her grasp. "Jesus, Carla. We gotta be careful."

Carla walked ahead of him, slid her hand into the back pockets of her tight jeans and pulled out the key to the Buick. She turned and held it out to Danny. "Here, you can drive."

He grabbed the keys. "We need to go by Jimmy's, get my tool bag."

She looked at him over the roof. "You left your bag at his apartment?"

Danny shook his head and opened the driver's side. He stepped into the Buick and leaned over, unlocked the passenger side for Carla. "It's in the trunk of the Caprice."

Carla slid over from her seat and put her hand on him.

Danny slouched down in the seat, put his hand on top of hers and showed her where to go. "We should wait till dark to go by Jimmy's." He gave her a look, ready to stop right there and pull his pants down to his ankles. But he turned the ignition and pulled out onto Baymeadow. He drove without paying much attention until he passed a Burger King. Carla still had her hand on him and he started to lose focus. His eyes jumped from one side of the road to the other, hoping he'd find a place with just enough privacy.

He knew it wouldn't take long.

But he turned left and headed north on Southside, drove a good mile then stopped in front of Jimmy's apartment.

Carla straightened out in her seat and pulled her hand back from his pants. "I thought we were going to wait until dark?"

He pulled into the parking lot and didn't answer. He drove slow past the Caprice and they both looked. But he continued through the parking lot and pulled around to the back of the building to the other side of the pond.

He stopped and put the car in park behind a big live oak. He could only see the top half of the building from where they were parked, no other cars around.

He turned off the ignition, and Carla crawled over to the driver's seat.

Her pants were already off.

Danny wrestled and got his pants down to his ankles. He had to do it with one hand and tried to ignore the pain in his wrist.

She crawled on top of him and he closed his eyes, leaned his head back. The evening sun reflected off the Spanish moss hanging from the tree.

22

SEAN PULLED THE cruiser into the parking lot of the Auburn Apartments. He scanned the lot for the maroon Caprice Jenna said she saw.

She pointed at the building. "There it is!"

Sean flipped on the lights. The Caprice was on the other side of the row from where they were. He slammed his foot on the gas and ripped the wheel around the last car and turned. But he had to jerk the wheel to avoid a Buick LeSabre parked in front of them. He drove around it and glanced at the woman in the passenger seat with her eyes on him through the window.

Sean stopped with the headlights on a man standing with his back to them, reaching into the trunk of the maroon Caprice.

The man turned and lifted his arm to shield his eyes, looking back into the cruiser's headlights.

Jenna turned to Sean. "That's him! The one who

jumped from the second floor!"

The man dropped a duffle bag on the ground and took off in the opposite direction across the lot. He ducked and disappeared between the parked cars.

Sean and Jenna both jumped out of the cruiser without a word. Sean heard the Buick's engine start but continued after the man. He yelled to Jenna just behind him. "Get the car!" He continued across the lot and cut out from the row of parked cars and stopped when the Buick's tires squealed and came right at him. He dove out of the way and hit the ground between the parked cars.

He jumped to his feet and watched the Buick drive toward the street. It jumped the curb and disappeared down Southside Boulevard, the headlights off.

The man turned the corner far ahead of Sean and headed into the woods behind the building.

Sean wasn't far behind, ran as fast as he could through the woods, with his hands out in front of him to avoid being whipped in the face by a branch.

He ran out from the woods and stopped, looked along the back exterior wall of a shopping center. He ran his eyes along the building and up toward the loading docks. There was a dumpster just ahead of him, up against the building's exterior.

Sean pulled out his Glock, walked toward the dumpster and pointed his gun when he heard a noise. He was careful with each step. His heart raced in his chest. Too many years to count had gone by since he was in pursuit. Especially on foot. He stepped closer and stood under the loading dock, wondering if the man had gone inside. The odor from the dumpster was strong and sharp.

He took a quick look behind him along the fence between the building and the woods. The only opening was the one he'd just run through, and he knew there was no way the man had escaped, unless he was inside. Or behind the dumpster just a few feet from where Sean stood. He looked up at the door next to the loading dock. It was open just a crack. He tucked his Glock in his holster and reached up, started to climb the concrete landing. But he heard a noise behind him and stopped. He pulled his gun again and turned toward the dumpster.

The door behind him creaked open, and the man jumped down from the loading dock and onto Sean's back. The two crashed to the asphalt, and Sean's gun fell from his hand. He tried to break loose and reach for the Glock, but before he could do a thing, he had a chain wrapped tight around his neck.

He tried to get it loose with both hands but he couldn't. It dug into his skin and squeezed his throat. He couldn't breathe. The pressure built up in his head. His face swelled, and he stumbled backward as the man pulled him from behind. But Sean let go of the chain and drove his elbows back, one after the other, and the chain loosened.

But only for a moment. The man fell back into the dumpster but didn't let go of the chain.

Sean dug his feet in but it only got tighter. He tried to stop from being pulled to the ground and swung his fists but couldn't connect. He tried to get his fingers between the chain and his throat.

Sean choked and turned his body, grabbed a fistful of the man's long hair. He somehow spun around enough to get his other hand out and had a clump of hair with both hands. He jerked the man to the ground and the chain loosened from his throat. He drove his knee into the man's chest and threw him on his back then reached down for his Glock.

He heard tires squeal and turned to look over his shoulder.

The Buick from the apartment parking lot came flying around the corner and drove straight for him. He had the Glock in his hand and raised it toward the driver. But the chain came down hard and smashed him on the wrist from behind. He somehow held on to the gun and turned to the man behind him then jumped in the air to avoid the oncoming car.

But it was too late.

He rolled up the hood and crashed into the windshield, flipped over the roof, and dropped hard to the ground.

He lay still on his back, and for a moment couldn't

move. He stared up into the dark sky then heard a door open and slam closed.

The car took off.

Sean still hadn't dropped his Glock. He forced himself to roll over onto his stomach and got into the prone position. He fired off a shot in the direction of the car, but it was already down at the other end of the building. His first shot missed. But he fired again and hit the rear brake light.

The car disappeared around the corner.

Sean rolled over again and stayed on his back. He wasn't sure what he'd broken. He stared up at the sky and tried to catch his breath then reached for the back of his head. He felt the warmth of his own blood.

The sheriff's cruiser came around the corner, blue lights on. Sean sat up, and Jenna slammed on the brakes, jumped from the car and ran toward him.

She crouched down next to him. "Are you shot?"

He rubbed his throat and shook his head, his elbows resting on his knees with his Glock still in his hand.

Jenna looked at the back of his head. "You're hurt," she said and clicked the two-way on her chest. "Officer injured at the scene behind Southside Square shopping center on Southside Boulevard." She helped Sean get up on one knee.

He looked along the building, shaking his head. It took him a moment but he got up on his feet. "You get a plate?"

She nodded. "They belong to a stolen Ford Focus."

Sean winced and reached for his ribs. He wondered if he'd broken one or two. It hurt to breathe. "She looked at me when we drove through the lot. I should've known they were together."

The sirens in the distance grew louder.

"I don't need the rescue... waste their time." He looked down at the chain on the ground, next to the dumpster. "That's twice I've had my ass kicked."

Jenna shook her head. "You got your *ass kicked* by a Buick LeSabre."

Sean stumbled and limped with each step.

"Maybe you should just lie down... wait for the rescue."

Sean shook his head. "Maybe Mac was right."

"Mac?"

"I'm too old for this shit." He turned and sat on the edge of the hood, reached for the back of his head, then looked at the blood on his fingers.

Jenna had her eyes on him. "It's different than being at the head of a classroom. But age has nothing to do with it. And it's not your usual week, start back on the streets and your own family's involved."

Sean pushed himself from the hood and walked around to the passenger side, pulled open the door, and slid inside. He turned and left the door open, his feet still outside the door.

A fire truck pulled around the corner and stopped behind them. An EMT vehicle drove around from behind it and parked next to Sean and Jenna's cruiser.

Sean stood up and waved them off. "I'm fine." He took another step from the car and stumbled. He grabbed on to the door to keep himself from hitting the ground.

Another sheriff's vehicle pulled in behind the rescue.

The med tech pulled a penlight flashlight from his shirt pocket, shined it into Sean's eyes. "You don't look fine," he said.

Sean took one more step and fell back into the door. He grabbed it with both hands and tried to focus his eyes. He nodded toward the black canvas bag in the man's hand. "I could use a Band-Aid."

Jenna stepped in front of Sean and stared back at him, then glanced at the medical technician. "You think you need to take him to get looked at?"

Sean rolled his eyes and gave her a look, about to open his mouth. But his legs gave out from under him. Jenna and the tech each grabbed an arm. A second tech came around from the back of the rescue with a stretcher.

Sean couldn't speak. He felt sick and his eyes closed.

23

CARLA PULLED THE Buick into the garage her ex-husband, Charles, owned. Danny sat in the passenger seat and held his wrist with more pain than he had before he got into it with the cop.

She turned off the ignition and stepped out from the driver's seat, walked outside the garage to where Charles stood, watching her from the driveway. Danny walked out behind her.

Charles looked her up and down, then turned his eyes inside the garage. "I don't like the idea of keeping this here. But I'll give you two days. You want my opinion, you'd be smart to just burn it, scrape the VIN. I know a guy, owns a chop shop..."

Danny shook his head. "Unh-uh. This was my grandmother's car."

Charles gave Danny a look. "Your grandmother's, huh? You'd rather keep granny's Buick, spend five to ten for running down a cop?"

"Leave him alone." Carla stared down at Charles. "It means something to him. I know you don't have that kind of heart, but..."

"No. He's right." Danny turned and stepped back to the car, ran his hand over the trunk's lid. "But it was the only thing she had left to her name when she died."

Carla held the keys up in front of her, dropped them into his hand. "Here, do what you think you should."

Danny removed one key—the one to Carla's apartment—and tossed them to Charles. "You can keep it, do what you want. I guess I owe you anyway."

Charles looked at the keys in his hand, then lifted his eyes to Danny. "When Carla told me you were the same kid used to hang around the Michelin Man, I thought maybe you'd be to Jerry's level of professionalism." He shook his head. "But Jerry'd never let a deal flop like you did, just wipe his hands clean and walk away." He laughed, a crooked smile on his face. "Then you give me this piece-of-shit car, like you're doing me a favor?" He shook his head. "Ain't worth twelve hundred bucks."

Danny stared back at him, didn't say a word.

Charles scratched the front of his balding head with his fingers, then he turned on a smile. "What you need to do is make it right."

Danny wasn't intimidated by Charles at all, but he

couldn't help but feel some respect for him. Maybe it was because Danny was banging Charles's ex-wife. "I never said I was going to walk away. But someone else stole them before we got there. So all I have to do is find out where they are."

Charles nodded. "I heard it took you two days just to pull your shit together, get over there. You gotta strike while the iron's hot. But you waited too long... you ask me." Charles shook his head, looked back at the Buick in the garage.

Danny looked at Carla, his eyebrows down over his narrowed eyes. "You told him I waited too long?"

Carla shook her head. "No, Danny, I didn't..."

"Don't push the blame on her, kid," Charles said. "She's not your mommy." Charles smiled and showed off his bleached-white teeth... a contrast from his tan, leathered face. He gave Carla a nod. "Although I guess she's old enough..." He laughed and turned, shaking his head. He looked back to Danny with a nod. "So this kid who took the paintings... he a friend of yours?"

Danny wanted to crack him, but he knew it wouldn't make things any better... blow the whole thing more than it was already blown. He took a moment before he answered. "He *was* a friend. But as soon as I find him..."

"You don't know where he is?" Charles said.

Carla said, "That's why we were at those

apartments when the cops showed up. Jimmy was about to be evicted and took off."

"Evicted, huh?" Charles stepped out of the garage and pulled down the door. "I've been desperate like that. Down to your last dime, do what you gotta do to dig yourself out of a hole." His expression dropped and he narrowed his eyes. "But I'd never screw over a friend to do it."

Danny stood quiet for a moment. "The artist's daughter was there when Jimmy went in the house, tied up the old lady. Even whacked a cop with a pipe... off-duty officer showed up out of the blue. Turns out he's the lady's nephew."

Charles put up his hand, his palm toward Danny. "Whoa, whoa, whoa. Wait a minute. You're telling me Richard Reed's nephew is a cop? And he was there when your buddy took those paintings?"

Danny nodded. "From what we've heard."

Charles pointed with his thumb at Danny, turned to Carla with a crooked smile on his face. "Where'd you find this kid?" He shifted his eyes back to Danny. "You mess with a cop's family, he doesn't sleep until he gets you. I don't care if you stole his little sister's candy or you shot his wife. It's personal." He walked up the steps toward his front door, stopped and turned, and looked around at his neighbor's houses. "Okay, so you don't know where to find your friend, and you don't know where to find the paintings. You're giving me a car worth maybe a thousand bucks, and I'm supposed to just forget the whole thing?" Charles shook his head, scratched his ear. "Tell me again, who's the girl?"

"She's Joseph and Nora Reed's daughter."

"The cop's cousin?"

Danny looked up the steps at Charles but didn't answer. He didn't have to.

Charles said, "At this point, you might be better off getting the hell out of here for a while. Go north. Go west. Just get out of Florida."

Danny looked at Carla, then stepped toward the bottom of the stairs. He looked up at Charles. "But what if I get you those paintings? Will you still keep your end of the bargain?"

Charles had already opened his front door but stopped and turned. He looked down the steps at Danny, then rubbed his face with both hands. "My end of the bargain?" He looked off, past them both. "I'll tell you what. You get me those paintings, I'll see what I can do. The buyer wasn't too pleased as you would imagine." He paused and scratched the front of his head. "I'll see what I can do. Maybe get you enough to disappear for good." He cracked half a smile, looked down at Carla. "Maybe go somewhere, get yourself a nice broad more your age."

Veronica pulled into the driveway in a small Chevy

S-10 pickup, one arm out the window like there wasn't enough room for her big body inside. She looked out at Danny and Carla. "Curtis got some plates this morning."

Carla got into the truck from the passenger side and slid over to the middle. Danny got in next to her and closed the door but didn't have much room. He leaned forward and looked at Veronica. She took up half the seat. He said, "Where's Curtis? With the girl?"

She took her eyes off the road for a moment and looked at Danny. "I've never had a hostage before... but it's not that big a deal. She doesn't even seem to mind being there."

Danny made a face. "Until she gets sick of grilled cheese."

Veronica leaned forward, her chin over the steering wheel. She stared out at the road. "I picked her up a pizza and a soda. She was pretty happy."

The three of them drove quiet for a couple of miles, Carla having to move her legs out of the way as Veronica shifted the manual stick on the floor.

Danny leaned forward again and looked at Veronica. "Hey, would you tell me the truth if you've talked to Jimmy?"

Veronica kept her eyes on the road and didn't answer.

He said, "You wouldn't keep something like that from me, would you?"

Carla put her hand on Veronica's big thigh. "It's okay, hon. I know you and Jimmy had a special relationship. But—"

"Special relationship?" Danny laughed. "He treated her like shit. He only treated her nice when he wanted her to put out... get his rocks off."

Carla turned to Danny, let out a sigh and stared into his eyes. "You think that's helpful?"

"What I'm saying is, we need to find Jimmy. Maybe we cut him back in if he's the one who really broke into that house... has those paintings hidden somewhere. He tries to sell them, word'll get out. Carla's ex will know. And he knows everyone in the business. Jimmy tries to sell them, Charles and his friends'll find out Jimmy's the one who screwed them..." He stopped, paused a moment. "We get to him first, we can make sure he doesn't get hurt. You know what I'm saying?" Danny kept his eyes on Veronica, but she stared straight out at the road. He looked at Carla. "Doesn't she hear me?"

They crossed the Main Street Bridge, headed north from San Marco.

Veronica finally opened her mouth and turned to Danny. She paused a moment. "Jimmy's staying at his sister's house, out in Lake City."

24

A NURSE WALKED into the room at Memorial Hospital and gave Sean a quick smile before she grabbed the clipboard hung on the foot of his bed. "The doctor will be in to see you shortly, hon." She turned for the door and walked out.

Detective Keith Riley walked in past her.

Sean felt pain in his neck and chest when he turned to Riley. "What are you doing here?"

Riley rolled his eyes. "Not even a 'Thanks for coming by?'"

Sean said, "I'm not in bad enough shape to need visitors."

Jenna was on the edge of his bed and stood up, folded her arms crossing her chest. "You find anything?"

Riley nodded. "That Caprice from the apartment is a match to the vehicle we picked up in the footage from Knight Street."

Sean tried to sit up a little more in bed and turn his body to Riley. "Where is it?"

"The Caprice? They're going through it now. No legal registration or any ID in the vehicle. VIN's been altered. Picked up the tool bag you said your assailant had in his hand when you first arrived at the apartment building. There was a pry bar in the bag, and there's a good chance we can trace it back to your aunt's house."

The three were quiet.

Riley gave Sean a nod. "So how's it feel? Not even a week on the streets and you're already getting in fights?"

Jenna held up two fingers. "Two fights."

Riley huffed a slight laugh.

Jenna said, "We're waiting for the X-rays and..."

The doctor walked into the room before she could finish. He walked to the end of the bed and looked at the clipboard, then slipped his hands into the pockets of his white coat. He gave Riley a nod then looked at Sean. "You have a concussion. But no broken bones."

Sean thought for a moment. "My head actually doesn't feel that bad. You sure I—"

"You threw up in the ambulance," Jenna said.

Sean gave her a look. "I did?"

The doctor nodded. "And you clearly have memory loss. Although we'd like to run you through an MRI, confirm there are no other issues." He glanced at Jenna. "Someone will be in soon to take him down."

Sean wanted to get up and walk out of there. But as he tried to sit up he felt a sharp pain shoot through his ribs. He leaned back against the pillow and took a moment before he spoke. He closed his eyes for a moment then looked up at Riley. "So we have no ID on the man who jumped from the apartment, but he's working with Jimmy Stanish. So all we have to do is find Jimmy. Hopefully that'll lead us to Gracie."

Riley nodded. "That was my exact thought. We're searching for him now. We understand he used to work at Raceway, over on Cassat Avenue."

Sean nodded. "Mac and I were there a few days ago. He loves their fried chicken."

Riley said, "Oh and we also ID'd Jimmy Stanish with footage from a 7-Eleven on West Union. Owner shot out the back window of a Buick LeSabre."

Jenna looked at Sean. "The same car... the woman from the apartment. She almost drove over Sean a couple of times."

Sean said, "I got a look at her but not good enough. Older than the kid I fought... maybe his mother or an older relative."

Riley said to Jenna, "Did *you* see her?"

"She was blonde, middle-aged. But other than that, I never saw her out of the car."

Riley said, "Jenna, if you're going back to the station after you leave here, let's see if we can find a match in the database... find this mysterious woman behind the wheel."

Jenna nodded and looked down at Sean as if to make sure he'd be okay if she took off. She rested her hand on his. "You'll be okay if I go, won't you?"

He stared up at her and nodded, then squeezed her hand as she started to step away. "The most important thing is we have to find Gracie. So no matter what, we can't let anything happen that'll put her in more danger than she's already in."

Jenna pulled her hand away and nodded. "We're going to find her, Sean. Don't worry."

Riley paused a moment, gave Jenna a look, then stepped toward the door. "They're on the run now. And we're a lot closer than we were... thanks to you and Jenna. We've got our ears on the ground in the black market. If, by chance, someone shows up with your uncle's art or it turns up out there, we'll have people waiting."

Sean was about to speak, but Mac walked through the door wearing jeans and a button-down shirt, untucked and hung well past his belt. "Didn't I tell you being on the streets would be different than teaching the young recruits?"

"Mac?" Sean had a surprised look on his face. He again tried to sit up in the bed but winced from the pain. "How'd you know I was here?"

"I was on the phone with Ward—nothing to do with you—told me you were run down in a parking lot at a shopping center." Mac gave Jenna a nod. "Officer Cash." He extended a hand to Riley next to him at the foot of the bed. "Hey, Riley. It's been awhile."

"What do you mean, it had nothing to do with me?" Sean said.

"Oh, well, we have a golf league. Just retired LEOs. Ward's not far away... thought I'd check on his plans." He cracked a crooked smile. "He's good with the irons." Mac's face turned serious. "He told me you were here." He paused a moment. "If there's anything I can do to help you or help find Gracie or... I mean... I know I don't have the badge, but it doesn't mean I can't help."

Sean nodded as a technician walked up behind Mac, lifted the sides up on Sean's bed. "You ready?"

Mac looked down at Sean. "Where are you going?"

The technician spoke up. "MRI."

Mac backed away from the bed. "Sean, I'm serious. You let me know what I can do." He put his hand on Sean's shoulder. "And you thought a kid knocking a box of chicken on a guy's lap was all the action you'd get?" He turned and walked from the room.

Sean pushed himself up, seated in the bed. "Mac. Wait. That kid..." He looked at Jenna. "The witness who had his leg broken in the car door at Raceway... he described him, right? Said he had long hair. And built... He was the one at the counter... at Raceway."

Mac turned back to Sean. "What are you saying? That's the same kid? How could..." The room went quiet.

Sean looked at Riley and Jenna. "Chief Hobson, from Fernandina Beach... his daughter worked behind the counter, serving chicken."

25

DANNY STEPPED PAST Carla and Veronica, reached his arm around and pulled out the .38 tucked in the waist of his pants. There was a burning smell in the hall outside Carla's apartment. The door was cracked open.

Danny lifted his foot and kicked the door. It swung and smashed open on the other side. He lifted the .38 in front of him and pointed it through the doorway.

Curtis turned from the stove, his hands raised up over his head. "Don't shoot!"

Danny took a breath and shook his head. He eased his gun down by his side, then tucked it back into his pants. "What the hell are you doing?"

"Making grilled cheese."

Carla brushed past Curtis and reached for the knob on the stove. "Where the hell'd you learn to cook? You're going to burn the whole place down, you keep it on high like that."

Danny stepped back and looked down the hall. "You check on her back there?"

Curtis nodded. "She's eating lunch."

Danny looked at the burnt grilled cheese in the pan. "Whose is that?"

Curtis shrugged. "It *was* mine, unless you want it?" He glanced at Veronica and she licked her lips, her eyes on the blackened creation smoking in the pan. He turned to Carla. "She asked if I had any weed, told her I'd ask you."

Carla nodded and reached into the cabinet next to the stove. "I'll hook her up if she—"

Danny put his arm out in front of Carla to stop her. "What the hell's this look like? She's a goddamn hostage... not a guest at Stoner Hotel."

Carla gave Danny a nod. "I thought you didn't want to be in the kidnapping business?"

"I don't." Danny reached into the pan and took a bite of the burnt grilled cheese, then dropped it back in the pan. He wiped his mouth with the back of his hand and made a face. He gave Curtis a look. "Christ, you can't even make grilled cheese?"

Carla ducked under Danny's arm and reached into the cabinet, pulled down a joint she'd already rolled earlier. "Can't hurt to get her high. Gotta be stressful having your hands shackled to a bed like that."

Curtis shook his head. "Well, actually... I let her have one loose, so she could eat."

Danny looked at the joint in Carla's hand. "Give her a few hits, you'd better make sure you tie up the other hand. We're not going to get relaxed with her at this point. Not until we figure out what we're going to do."

Curtis said, "What about Jimmy? I thought you were going to try to find him."

Danny nodded. "I am. But if we don't find the paintings, the more I think about it, maybe it's not such a bad idea... tell the old lady to pay if she wants to see her daughter again."

Curtis sat down at the table next to Veronica. "You don't know where he is?"

"Jimmy?" Danny nodded. "He's out at his sister's... in Lake City."

"You talk to him yet?"

"No." Danny still had his eyes on Veronica. "And I'd appreciate it if nobody else does."

Danny was alone behind the wheel, turned the Chevy S-10 down Forest Street toward 95, then headed west on 90. He drove past the sign, Welcome to Lake City, Florida's Gateway.

He should've known Jimmy would go hide at his sister's place. Besides Danny, he didn't have many friends.

He turned the wheel and pulled into the driveway, parked just outside the carport with the Lincoln

Town Car parked underneath. It didn't look like it'd been driven in a while, faded paint and at least two flat tires. The house looked like every other house on the street, all thrown up by the same builder, or maybe just dropped off a truck. Looked as much like a long trailer as it did a regular house.

The yard was covered in mostly tall weeds, everything overgrown in a decent-sized lot surrounded by oaks. The branches overhung the roof with six seasons of leaves piled in the gutters.

Danny straightened out his shirt, felt for his snub-nosed .38 tucked in the back of his pants. He didn't like to stick his piece in front of his pants, ever since Jerry told him about a cousin who shot his own dick off.

He stepped under the carport and looked inside the Lincoln. The back seat was filled with magazines and empty soda cans. A blue tarp caught his eye in the backyard, thrown over what looked to Danny like Jimmy's van.

There were no other cars around, other than the Lincoln with the two flat tires. He knew it wasn't going anywhere. He wondered if anybody was home.

He walked back to the front of the house. His heart pounded in his chest... and he wasn't sure if it was his nerves or adrenaline.

He pulled open the white aluminum storm door and knocked hard with his knuckles on the wooden door. Curtains covered the door's windows, so he couldn't see inside. He leaned over the black metal railing and looked through the window just off to the right.

He heard a TV but couldn't see anyone. He knocked again, turned and looked back at the road. A car drove by and blew the horn. He turned back when the lock clicked.

The door opened.

A pretty young woman, no more than twenty with long hair and a Def Leppard T-shirt cut off at the belly stood in the doorway. She had a baby in her arms, and they both stared out at Danny.

Danny's eyebrows went high up on his head. "You had a baby?"

She didn't answer him. "What are you doing here, Danny?"

He hesitated a moment, his eyes still on the baby. "Maggie, tell me where he is."

She turned and looked back into the house, then back to Danny. "Where is *who*?"

"Don't play games with me, Maggie. Tell me where he is." His eyes went back to the baby. "What's his name?"

"She's a *she*. Her name's April."

"Whose is it?"

Maggie rolled her eyes. "Ain't seen you around in a long time."

Danny nodded, looked out toward the street

himself to see what she was looking at. His eyes went back to Maggie's then past her, into the house. "I need to talk to Jimmy."

Maggie looked at Danny's shoes. "I don't know what happened with you two, but I don't want any part of it. I already told Jimmy he can't stay here."

The baby started to cry, and Maggie bounced her up and down on her hip. She rested her gentle hand on the baby's face and looked up at Danny. "I got a little girl now. Don't need no trouble in my life. And I certainly don't want her to—"

"Maggie, your brother took something that belongs to me. And I can't help but think you know exactly what I'm talking about." He looked toward the side of the house. "That's his van back there, isn't it?"

She shook her head. "Honest, Danny. Jimmy don't tell me nothin'."

"Then tell me where he is." He looked into the house. "Tell him to come out here."

She didn't flinch or say another word.

But Danny'd had enough. He reached around behind him, came out with the .38 in his hand. He pointed it at Maggie. "Let's go. Inside."

Maggie didn't scream or yell or seem to show much fear at all. "Please don't hurt my baby, Danny. That's all I'm askin' from you." She looked down into the muzzle then turned and walked into her house.

Danny followed behind her. His eyes bounced around. "I ain't gonna hurt her. You neither. As long as you either tell him to come out from wherever he's hiding. Or get him on that phone if you know how to reach him." His eyes went to the coffee table and the bottle of ketchup sitting there. He turned off the television. "Jimmy? I know you're in here. Get your ass out here. Stop being such a pussy and show your face."

The baby again started to cry.

Maggie held her baby closer, pulled her head into her chest. "You're scaring April, Danny." She walked into the kitchen.

Danny tucked the .38 back in his pants and followed behind her.

She picked up a phone and pulled a piece of paper from a drawer. "He has a new cell phone. New number. I'll call him, find out where he is."

Danny took a step closer, looked at her screen and saw she'd dialed 9-1-1.

He ripped the phone from her hand and grabbed her by the crux of her arm. He spun her and got right in her face, then looked at the crying baby and let go of Maggie's arm. "Why you being so stupid, Maggie? You gonna call the cops on me? I haven't done shit... so what the hell you gonna tell them?" He took the piece of paper from her hand. "Is this his number?"

The baby's cry got louder.

Danny dialed the number from the paper. "Feed that kid or something, will you?" He handed her the phone. "Tell him he doesn't get here in five minutes, you'll be the one in trouble."

Maggie put the phone up to her ear, and Danny heard a phone ring somewhere in the house. He grabbed the phone out of Maggie's hand and put it up to his ear, pulled his gun from his pants and walked toward the ringing. He growled. "Jimmy? Where the hell are you?"

A door swung open from down the hall and Jimmy ran at Danny, dropped his shoulder, slammed and knocked him down on his back. He smashed through the aluminum storm door, snapped it right off the hinges. The door landed on the concrete steps and Jimmy jumped over it.

Danny jumped up and ran out behind him, through the doorway and down the steps... ran across the street and into the neighbor's yard. He held the gun up on Jimmy. "Don't make me put one of these in your back!"

Jimmy's foot caught on a railroad tie bordering the neighbor's flower garden, and he fell flat on his face.

Danny stood over him, breathing heavy with his .38 pointed down at Jimmy's head.

Jimmy turned over and held his hands out in front of him. "Danny, don't. I'm sorry. I really am."

Danny kept the gun on Jimmy. "Tell me what you did with those goddamn paintings."

"Okay. Okay. Just put the gun away. You don't need it. I'll show you what I have." Jimmy got up on his feet.

Danny shoved him toward Maggie's house, walked across the street with the .38 in Jimmy's back. He saw Maggie watching from inside the doorway, the baby no longer in her arms. But Danny could hear the crying from somewhere inside the house.

Danny walked Jimmy up the driveway and past the Lincoln under the carport. He looked at the van. "You better tell me you didn't sell any of 'em. 'Cause if you did..."

"You think I'd be sleeping on my sister's couch if I did?" Jimmy stepped up to the back of the van, flipped the tarp up onto the roof and reached into his pocket, came out with a set of keys. He unlocked the rear doors, pulled them open, then stepped back out of Danny's way.

Danny looked inside at the paintings with a bedsheet thrown over the top and leaned up against the walls of the van. He tucked his .38 in the back of his pants and stepped inside. He reached for the closest painting. "You know, I wouldn't have had to..." He turned and looked toward the open door. Jimmy wasn't there. "Jimmy?" He pulled his pistol from his pants and stepped out with one foot on the ground.

Jimmy had the cop's Glock 22 held on Danny.

But before Jimmy said a word, Danny lifted the .38

and pulled the trigger three times.

Jimmy dropped the Glock to the ground. He reached for his throat with both hands. Blood came through his fingers and dripped down his arm.

Danny popped off one more shot, not even sure where it hit him.

Jimmy's blood-covered hands slid off his throat. He stared back at Danny and opened his mouth. But no words came out. He choked and gagged. He fell to his knees then dropped, facedown, into the overgrown weeds in Maggie's backyard.

Danny stared down at Jimmy for a moment, then stepped up into the van and wrapped his arms around three of the paintings. He hopped down from the van and moved as fast as he could. But the damn paintings were heavier than he'd expected. He made it across the yard and walked past the Lincoln under the carport. One painting slid from his grasp and the corner of the frame cracked on the ground. "Shit." He let it fall but kept moving, put the two he had in the back of the Chevy, picked the one up he'd dropped, then hurried back to the van.

After a handful of trips he had them all in the back of the truck. He didn't look back at the house.

He heard sirens and knew Maggie called the cops. He climbed into the front seat and turned the key, shifted into drive, and squealed the tires. Almost up on two wheels, he turned left onto Justin Glenn with the pedal to the floor. The paintings all crashed in the back. The sirens grew louder, but he drove in the other direction and watched in the rearview. He turned and looked over his shoulder, saw the sheet Jimmy had wrapped around the paintings blow out the back. It landed in someone's yard.

Danny drove fast. As fast as the truck would go but the engine didn't seem to like it.

He saw a dirt road, wasn't sure if it was someone's driveway but turned down it anyway. At least it got him off the main road. He bounced up and down in the seat. Dust trailed behind him and he kept going for at least half a mile. Didn't appear to be private property but he didn't care. He was far enough from the road, and when he felt he was in the clear, turned off the engine and waited.

26

"I'M NOT PAYING anybody a ransom." Nora stared straight ahead then turned and looked at Sean, seated next to her on the couch. "What kind of money do you think I have?"

He was surprised she took her time getting back from Maine after her home had been broken into and her daughter had disappeared. Although nothing Nora said or did ever surprised many people. "I'm not saying you'll have to," he said. "There's been no demand. But we're not exactly sure if they'll come forward at some point. In fact, for obvious reasons... we hope they do. And we'd like to be prepared."

Nora looked off in the distance. "You just need to do your job and find her." She shifted her eyes toward the baby grand. "Of course, I'd like to get those paintings back. But you already let whoever it was that took them slip out of here." She looked across the room at Jenna, standing by the front door.

"He couldn't even stop the man, standing there in front of him."

Sean got up from the couch and turned back to Nora. "Whoever broke in expected to find those paintings. If it was the same man, then he must've thought there were more. If it was someone else, well..." He glanced over at Jenna then back to Nora. "We don't believe they came here for Gracie. It appears she just happened to be in the wrong place at the wrong time."

Nora gave him a look. "That's always been her excuse." She paused a moment. "But I still don't understand how anyone knew about the paintings. It's not like Joseph was some famous artist..."

"He actually was," Sean said. "And you were interviewed on the news. Didn't we talk about this already?"

Jenna stepped toward Sean and Nora and nodded at the photo in Nora's hand. "If you would look at the photo again, try and remember if he's the same man who came here and tied you up."

Nora studied the photo, her eyes squinted. She looked up at Jenna and handed it back to her. She shrugged. "I already told you, his face was covered. So I don't know what you want me to tell you."

"You said he had a beard."

She nodded. "Coming out from under his mask. I told you that already." She looked up at Sean. "You're the one who should've gotten a better look at him, if you knew how to fight." Her face got somewhat twisted. "And I don't know what makes you think the same person would come here a second time." She shook her head and stood up from the couch.

Jenna said, "That's what we're trying to determine... whether or not he's the one who came back here. It doesn't make a lot of sense, unless he was hoping to find more paintings. That would explain why someone was in the attic."

She nodded. "And ruined my ceiling."

Sean got a call from Riley on his way back to the station.

Riley said, "Jimmy Stanish is dead. Shot in his sister's backyard, out in Lake City."

Sean glanced at Jenna with the phone up to his ear. "Riley, let me put you on speaker. Jenna's right here, behind the wheel." He tapped the screen and held the phone out between them. "Can you repeat that one more time?"

"Jimmy Stanish was shot and killed out at his sister's house in Lake City. Shot three times. Got 'im in the neck with a .38."

Sean said, "Any witnesses?"

"His sister was the only one in the house, with her baby. Said she didn't see or hear a thing."

"You believe her?"

Riley paused a moment. "If she was deaf and blind, maybe."

Sean turned and looked out the passenger window.

Riley said, "Either of you know the name Danny Womack?"

Sean looked back at Jenna.

She said, "Is he the young kid used to hang around Jerry Russo?"

Riley said, "He's not exactly a kid. But, yeah, that's him. Did some time for a job he did for Russo. But Russo skated. Jimmy was said to be involved but was never able to pull it together. Womack paid the price."

Sean looked down at the phone. "Anything else we should know?"

"His body was in the back of the house, next to a van covered with a tarp. Rear doors wide open."

Jenna and Sean gave each other a look. "White van?"

"Looked to be from the cable company, or at least a contractor with them. Had a magnetic sign on the side, but we called the cable company and it's not theirs."

Sean said, "Sounds like the same van Jimmy had been spotted in, more than once." He thought for a moment. "You have an address?"

Riley went quiet for a moment. "Uh, actually... Captain Ward asked me to tell you to come in... said he needs to talk to you before you go anywhere you're not supposed to."

Sean thought for a moment. "Why wouldn't he just call me himself? You his messenger now?"

"Just go see him when you get to the station. All right?" Riley hung up without another word.

Sean looked up from the phone and toward the road. "I'd like to have someone keep an eye on my aunt. If Danny Womack has Gracie... you never know if he'll use her to get money." He turned to Jenna. "To be honest, I wasn't worried about Gracie at first. I thought she was somehow involved. I couldn't think of any other reason why she came back down to Florida other than to get her hands on her father's paintings."

Jenna gave him a quick look. "And now?"

He took a moment before he answered. "I'd be lying if I said I wasn't worried."

Jenna paused a moment. "She'll be all right, Sean. We'll find her."

"But we need to be realistic. If he has no problem shooting his childhood friend..."

Jenna turned the cruiser into the station and turned off the engine. They both sat still for a moment.

Sean reached for the door's handle. "Gracie's tough. That's one thing she has going for her. Something she got from her mother. I don't think she has much fear in her." He turned and looked at Jenna. "That might be the only good thing she got from Nora." He pushed open the door. "I don't care what the captain tells me. I'm going to find Gracie." He stepped out and closed the door. "If I wanted to sit back and do nothing... I would've stayed in the academy."

27

DANNY STORMED INTO Carla's apartment, breathing heavy, with his eyes wide open. He stared at Carla with her bare feet up on the coffee table. She leaned back and took a hit from her joint.

He looked around the apartment. "Where is everyone?"

"Curtis went out to get another car."

"What about Veronica?"

Carla shrugged, the smoke rolling off the joint between her long fingers. "She went with him, I guess."

Danny cocked his head back. "You guess?"

She licked the tips of her fingers and squeezed the lit end of the joint, put it down on the coffee table in front of her. She moved forward and sat on the edge of the couch. She turned and looked up at Danny. "Are you going to tell me how it went?"

Danny hesitated before he answered. "I got the

paintings, if that's what you're asking me." He looked down along her legs. "Get some shoes on, help me carry them up."

Carla tilted her head. "You're bringing them in here?"

"What the hell else am I supposed to do with them?"

She took her time but finally stood up from the couch. "You should bring them to Charles, let him take a look. Maybe he'll let you keep them in his garage."

Danny thought for a moment, then turned and took a can of Pabst Blue Ribbon out of the refrigerator. He cracked the top and emptied half the can down his throat.

Carla walked in behind him. "So you and Jimmy made up?"

Danny gave her a look over the top of his can as he took another swig. He held his mouth full of beer, his cheeks puffed out like a hamster before he finally swallowed. He stepped up to the sink and finished the rest of the can with his back to Carla, then crushed it with one hand, tossed it on the counter. "What's up with the girl back there?"

"She's asleep, last I looked."

"Asleep? What'd you... get her stoned?"

Carla didn't answer.

He said, "She's not your new girl-toy, you know. She's a goddamn hostage." He turned and walked out the door and headed for the stairs. He yelled over his shoulder, "Let's go!" He was halfway down the stairs and stopped, turned, and yelled up at Carla. "Hurry up, will you? We gotta get this truck out of here."

Carla turned the corner and followed him down the stairs and down to the truck. She stopped at the tailgate and Danny reached over and into the truck bed, turned, and handed her two paintings.

"Jesus," she said. "They're heavy." She rested them both down on the ground and looked down at the painting facing out to her. "Can't imagine this one's worth a whole lot of money. Looks like a five-year-old painted it."

"What the hell do you know?" Danny gave her a look, then reached over and into the back of the truck. He wrapped his arms around three paintings, lifted them out and headed for the stairs.

Carla lifted the two paintings and started to follow behind him. "I know more than you might think." She stopped. "I can't carry both of these at once. I'll come back for the second one." She put one of the paintings back inside the truck's bed, picked up the other and walked up the stairs.

He continued up the stairs and didn't answer until he stopped on Carla's floor, just outside her door. He lifted his foot and pushed it open, stepped through the kitchen and leaned the paintings down against the wall in the living room. He wiped his hands together and turned to the window. He looked down toward the truck. Carla walked in with one painting in her arms and he said, "Jimmy's dead."

Carla put the painting down with her eyes on Danny, moved a strand of hair back from her face. "Jimmy's dead? What do you mean *he's dead?*"

"What other meaning would there be?" He shrugged. "He's dead." He walked past her back out the door of her apartment. He headed for the stairs.

Carla came after him and grabbed him by the back of his shirt. "Danny? What the fuck?"

He continued down the stairs as if she wasn't holding on to him. She let go, and he walked out to the truck, grabbed three more paintings. He turned and brushed past Carla. "Keys are in the ignition," he said. "Go ahead and move it around the other side of the fence." He took a couple more steps then turned and looked down at Carla, staring up at him. "What are you waiting for?" he said. "Move the truck, will you?" He walked up the rest of the way and leaned back into the door. He walked across the kitchen and laid the paintings down with the others.

Carla walked in behind him carrying one painting.

Danny took the painting from her hands, leaned it down with the others. "You move the truck, like I told you?" He nodded toward her phone on the coffee table. "Call Charles, see if you can get him over here." He looked down along the paintings. "Let's hope something here's worth a few coins."

Carla grabbed him by the arm. "Danny... what did you do?"

He pulled his phone from his pocket, kneeled down in front of one of the paintings and took a picture. He acted like Carla hadn't said a word. He looked at his phone, then straightened out and shifted his eyes to Carla. "He pulled a gun on me." He squinted his eyes and nodded his head with a shrug. "I shot him."

Carla gasped, put both hands over her mouth.

Danny rolled his eyes. "Christ, the weed making you all dramatic now?" He looked outside. "His sister was there. That's where I've been."

"With his sister?"

He shook his head. "No. I was hiding from the cops."

"She called them?"

Danny shrugged. "I assume so. Seen her brother get shot right there in her own backyard..."

"She saw it?"

Danny thought for a moment, remembered he didn't see her anywhere. And didn't look for her... just got the hell out of there as fast as he could. "I don't know what she saw."

Carla looked him up and down. "You seem pretty calm for someone who just killed his best friend."

Danny made a face. "Best friend? I told you, he pulled the gun on me first. It was self-defense."

Carla gave him a look, somewhat sympathetic,

stepped toward Danny and wrapped her arms around him. She rested her hand on the back of his head. "I'm so sorry, babe."

Danny pushed her away. "Wasn't for him we wouldn't be in this mess in the first place. Never would have been pinched, either... spent those years eating prison food while he was living his life on the outside."

"What are you going to do? What if the sister saw you?"

"She knew I was there. But she can't say for sure I was the one who pulled the trigger. She probably couldn't see from inside the house, where me and Jimmy stood. He had his van back there, covered in a blue tarp. Paintings were inside."

"You sure the cops are looking for you?"

Danny didn't answer, looked down at the paintings along the wall. "Will you just call Charles, get him over here?" He reached out and grabbed her, pulled her into him, and squeezed her ass. "We get what I'm hoping, we can finally get the hell out of this steaming shithole for good."

Carla was gentle as she pushed him away with both hands against his chest. "*We?*"

"Curtis and Veronica get their cut. Me and you get ours, maybe head West like Charles said we should."

Carla grabbed the phone from the coffee table, turned and walked down the hall.

"Carla."

She stopped and looked back at him.

He said, "Why's she so quiet back there?" He walked away without waiting for her answer and opened the fridge, pulled out another can of beer. He sat down at the table and cracked the top, then pulled out his phone. He was about to dial Curtis, but his mind went to Maggie. He knew he should've gone to talk to her without leaving the house. Tell her it was just an accident... maybe say Jimmy shot himself.

28

IT WAS LATE when Sean pulled up in front of the house in Lake City. He parked the Explorer on the street and walked up the driveway, noticed the Lincoln Town Car with two flat tires parked under the carport. He didn't see any other cars. He looked around the yard and walked along the concrete walkway. He stood on the bottom step and looked down at an aluminum storm door leaned up against the side of the house.

A baby cried inside, and he walked up the stairs, knocked on the door, and waited.

After a few moments, he knocked again. The door opened, and a young woman with a can of Miller Lite in her hand looked out at him but didn't say a word.

"Maggie?"

She took a moment, then nodded and looked out at his Ford. "Something I can help you with?"

"I'm Officer Sean Coyle, with the Jacksonville Sheriff's Office." He showed her the badge he had hooked on his belt.

Her eyes went to the badge. She looked out at his Explorer again and sipped her beer. "Officers don't wear uniforms in Jax?"

"I'm off duty." He turned and looked out at the street, just to be sure he was outside alone. "I'm sorry about your brother."

"Oh? Well, I ain't gonna talk about that no more. I answered every question I could and was told that would be it for today."

Sean kept his eyes on her and forced out a smile. "Your brother had something to do with my cousin." He paused a moment. "She's missing, and we're trying to find her." He looked down at the concrete under his feet. "I'm sure you loved your brother. But I need your help."

Maggie stepped outside onto the concrete landing in front of Sean. There wasn't much room between them. "I'm sorry," she said. "But I don't see how I can help. Jimmy wasn't the type to be into kidnapping, if that's what you're saying... taking little girls."

The baby had stopped crying and Maggie turned, looked through the open door. "I could tell you... he loved his niece." She brushed a strand of hair from her face. "He wouldn't hurt a girl, I can tell you that."

"Actually, she's a grown woman."

"Oh."

"She happened to be in the wrong place at the wrong time." He paused a moment. "Your brother stole paintings from her mother's house, and my cousin Gracie happened to be home when it happened."

Maggie sat down on the top step and sat quiet for a moment.

Sean stepped past her and down onto the concrete walkway. He tried to look her in the eye. "Do you know anything about it?"

Before she could answer, the baby started to cry. Maggie's shoulders dropped as she shook her head with her eyes closed for a moment. She stood up from the step and walked inside. "Shit, I'm sorry. I gotta get my baby." She took a few steps, then stopped and turned toward the door. She held up her can of beer and shook it. "Can I get you a drink?"

Sean was about to say no, but then gave her a warm smile and nodded. "Sure. I'll have a beer if you've got an extra one?" He thought if he could get her to relax, let her guard down, she'd be willing to tell him what she knew.

Maggie came out a few moments later with a baby in her arms and a beer in each hand. She handed one to Sean, then looked down at the baby. "This here is April." She kissed the little girl on her forehead. "She doesn't like to sleep much in the evening." She sipped her beer and looked off into the darkening sky. "Wish she would... Mamma needs her alone time, you know."

"How old is she?"

"She'll be two in March."

Maggie didn't have a ring on her finger, and without asking, he assumed she'd raised her baby all alone. She was a kid herself, barely over twenty-one is what he'd learned.

"You were here when your brother..." He looked down at the baby in Maggie's arms and stopped before he asked the question.

Maggie shrugged. "You can say what you want around April. There ain't much she hasn't heard already."

"I... I was just confirming you were here when it happened. But I understand you didn't see anything?"

She shook her head. "No, sir, I was with April at the time. Giving her a bath."

"You didn't hear anything? The gunshot?"

She shook her head but didn't exactly answer.

Sean didn't buy it at all. Although he'd never spent much time around a screaming baby, he couldn't imagine how she'd miss the sound of three pops from a .38. "You know a man who was friends with your brother... name's Danny Womack?"

Maggie stared back at him and didn't shift her eyes

in the least... didn't even flinch when Sean said Danny's name. She shook her head. "Never heard the name. Been a while since I moved out this way, haven't even seen Jimmy in a couple of years. He only started coming around lately 'cause he needed a place to sleep. That's how he was..."

Sean stared back at her, then looked off into the darkness around the yard. He thought for a moment, then turned back to her, glanced over her shoulder and into the house. He slapped his arm, like he'd been bitten by a bug of some sort. "Bugs are nasty tonight. You mind if we go inside?"

Maggie paused a moment, then shifted her baby from one hip to the other. "I wouldn't mind seeing if April'll go back to sleep." She turned and walked in the door, then looked over her shoulder at Sean. "Lake City PD already went through the place... if there's something in particular you might be looking for."

Sean walked in behind her. "Would it be okay if I used your bathroom?"

She paused a moment, then nodded down the hall straight ahead of where she stood. "Right down over there." She walked down the hall ahead of him, reached into the bathroom, and turned on the light. "I'm going to see if I can put April down." She backed away, then walked through the next door on the right, turned and closed it behind her.

Sean looked at the framed photos hung on the

wall. One of them caught Sean's eye, and he looked toward the closed door Maggie had walked through, made sure she wasn't about to come out. He looked closer at the photo of Maggie and the man he knew was Jimmy. There was another man on the other side of Maggie... one he recognized right away. It was the same man from Jimmy's apartment... the one who had attacked him behind the shopping center, nearly choked him to death.

29

DANNY SAT AT the table under the window in Carla's apartment, empty cans of Pabst Blue Ribbon spread out in front of him with a half bottle of Jim Beam. He sat quiet with his eye on the window, the .38 in his hand hanging over the back of the chair.

There was a knock at the door.

He wasn't even ten steps away, right there in the kitchen, but yelled for Carla to get the door.

She came from down the hall with an empty plate in her hand and gave Danny a look. "You couldn't get it?" She leaned into the door and looked through the peephole. "It's Charles."

Carla opened the door and Charles walked past her. He sniffed into the air. "Still smoking the weed, huh?" He looked toward Danny, then shifted his eyes to all the empty cans of beer. "Jesus Christ," he said. "My old man used to drink that shit. Put back about a twelve pack by the third inning of a Yankees' game." He laughed. "They lose, the belt would come out..."

Danny closed one eye, just so he could focus a little better. He raised a can of beer to Charles, as if to toast him, then tipped his head back and finished what was inside. He crushed the can with one hand and stood from the chair... stumbled with his first step but grabbed onto the edge of the counter and caught himself. He waved his hand in the air for Charles to follow him into the other room. "Come on, let me show you."

Charles walked in behind Danny, looked down at the paintings leaned up against the wall.

There was another knock at the door. Danny gave Carla a nod. "Let them in, will you?" He still had the .38 in his hand. "And keep it quiet about Jimmy."

Charles looked up from the paintings when Curtis walked into the room. Veronica walked in next and Charles's eyes opened wide. He looked up at her, the top of his head not even to her chin. "Jesus..."

Veronica gave him a look, then shifted her eyes toward the paintings. She turned to Danny. "You got them from Jimmy?"

Danny nodded but looked away. "Unh-huh."

She looked around the room and glanced down the hall. "He didn't come back here with you?"

Danny shook his head.

"What'd he say?"

Danny didn't answer, needed to focus... make sure he didn't say something he didn't want to. Without thinking, he stuck his .38 in the front of his pants.

Charles didn't pay any of them much attention. He crouched down, pulled out a magnifying glass and held it in his hand over one of the paintings. He looked up at Danny. "These damaged like this when you got 'em?"

Danny shrugged. "Been moved around a lot, I guess."

Charles kept his eyes on Danny for a moment then back down to the paintings. He stood up, his eyes a bit squinted, looking at each painting along the wall. He scratched the top of his balding head and turned to Danny. "So where are the rest of 'em?"

Danny glanced at Curtis, took a moment before he answered Charles. "This is it."

Charles gave Carla a look. "Is he serious?"

Danny clenched his jaw and stepped up to Charles. "Why you asking her? You can't look me in the eye, you want to get smart like that?" Danny had that look in his eye... the one his mother used to say was the devil coming through him.

Charles folded his arms across his chest, just under where his man boobs poked through his silk-like T-shirt. "What I mean, Danny boy, is you're two sheets to the wind." He looked him up and down and shook his head. He huffed through his nose. "Look at him. Can barely stand." He turned to Carla.

"There may be paintings worth real money..." He paused a moment and looked out at the blue sky through the window. "But these ain't them."

Danny felt for the .38 in his pants.

Carla grabbed his arm and looked him in the eye. Her lips barely moved. "Don't you *dare*..."

Charles looked down at Danny's hand, the .38 in his grasp but still in his pants. "I'd appreciate it, you keep that thing in there." He glanced at Carla as if Danny wasn't even there. "He's gonna shoot me now? For telling him like it is?"

Curtis and Veronica gave each other a look, backed out of the room and disappeared into the kitchen.

Danny glanced from Carla to Charles. He pulled the gun from his pants and let it hang in his hand by his side.

Charles shook his head and walked out of the room and into the kitchen. Danny followed him and turned the corner as Charles started for the door.

Danny lifted the .38 and pointed it right at Charles. "Where you think you're going?"

Curtis jumped up from the table. "Christ, Danny... what the hell are you doing? He's here to help us." He reached for Danny's arm. "Put it away."

Carla walked past Danny and stood between him and Charles.

Danny broke out laughing. He tucked the .38 in his pants, this time in the waistband around his back. His laugh didn't stop. He was almost hysterical.

Everyone else was quiet.

Danny reached for the bottle of Jim Beam from in front of Veronica at the table, shaking his head. Still laughing. "I just wanted to see if the old man would piss his pants." He looked over at Charles in front of the door. "You're a tough bastard, huh? Not afraid of getting shot?"

Carla pulled the bottle of Jim Beam from Danny's hand. "You've had enough to drink."

Charles's face was beet red, still not saying a word with his hand on the doorknob. He didn't seem to find any of it funny at all. He looked at Carla. "This isn't how I do business, sweetie." His eyes moved to Danny. "If it wasn't for Carla, I wouldn't even be talking to you. You'll get pennies on the dollar for these paintings... trying to sell 'em on ebay."

Danny lifted his chin and looked down over his nose toward Charles, with his shoulders back, arms hung loose behind him... a look he'd picked up as a kid watching Dennis Quaid in the Jerry Lee Lewis movie. "I told you I was just messing around." He put his arm around Charles's shoulder and led him back into the other room. "Would you just take another look? These are the only ones we got. I don't know about the other paintings. We couldn't find them in the old lady's house."

Charles slid out from under Danny's arm but continued back into the room with the paintings. He pulled out his magnifying glass again, crouched down in front of the same painting he had before. "This one here's worth, maybe, a couple grand." He looked back and forth at the others. "These"—he stood up, scratched his head—"a grand a piece, if you're lucky."

Danny slammed his hand onto his forehead and ran it through his long hair, squeezed his eyes tight, and shook his head. "Wait... wait." He shook his head. "No. No way. That ain't right." He looked back at Curtis. "You said these were worth a hundred grand." He pointed with his thumb toward Charles. "He's telling me we're lookin' at, what..." He looked at the paintings, bobbed his head up and down as he tried to do the math. "Curtis, what's that come to?"

Curtis had his phone in his hand, his eyes down on the screen. He pulled an image up on his phone and turned it to Charles. "This one's worth six figures."

Charles stared at Curtis's phone, then ran his eyes along the paintings. He looked from one painting to the next, shook his head and turned back to Curtis. "You see it here? 'Cause I don't. All I see is *shit*." He paused a moment and rubbed the loose skin on his neck. "Ten grand for the whole lot. And that's being generous."

Veronica hadn't spoken a word since she walked in the door, walked in and out of the kitchen with a little yellow bag of potato chips in her hand, sticking one after another in her mouth.

Danny looked directly at her, then down at the

paintings. He kept his eyes down for a moment then lifted them back to Veronica. He twisted his mouth, chewed the inside of his cheek, then for no good reason came out and said it. "I shot Jimmy."

30

JENNA SAT ACROSS from Sean and Detective Riley in the kitchen at the station and flipped through papers in a long manila folder. "Daniel J. Womack," she said. "Born in Towson, Maryland, but moved to Jax to live with his grandmother when he was eight. She's now deceased." Her eyes moved along the page. "Has a cousin out in Oakland and one in Georgia." Jenna continued. "Jerry Russo might be the closest he had to a relative. At least in Jax."

Sean said, "He the one you said was called the *Michelin Man?*"

Riley spoke up. "Jerry Russo's responsible for at least seventy-five B&Es in Northeast Florida. Did a couple of bank jobs but that wasn't his thing. Slippery bastard..."

Jenna placed the papers down on the table. "Weighed three hundred pounds when he died."

Sean got up and walked to the coffee machine. He poured himself a cup and leaned back against the counter next to the sink. "There's gotta be a reason Jimmy's sister won't finger Womack. She wouldn't even admit she knew him... even though she's got a photo of him on her wall, right there for anyone to see."

"I'm sure she's scared," Jenna said.

Sean took a sip from the Styrofoam cup and made a face, dumped the contents down the sink, and dropped the cup in the wastebasket.

Jenna looked up at Sean from the table. "Captain made it clear... Lake City PD's in charge. So our hands are somewhat tied for now."

Sean sat down next to her and looked across at Riley. "You believe they can't find a single fingerprint in that van that doesn't belong to Stanish?"

Riley nodded. "They always seem to be backed up over there. We offered to help, but as usual they declined any assistance." He scratched the top of his head. "They're so goddamn understaffed..."

Sean leaned back in the chair with his arms folded, his feet out straight beneath the table. "I have to get out there, talk to Maggie again before something happens. We had a pretty good rapport. Maybe I'll bring her a six of Miller Lite."

Jenna stood up from the table and grabbed a bottle of water from the refrigerator.

Riley leaned on the table, his hands folded in front

of him with his eyes on Sean. "You can't go out there again. Ward finds out and..."

Sean gave Riley a look, his eyes somewhat narrowed. "He's not going to find out. *Right?*" He turned and looked out the window, toward the parking lot. "I know we have to nail Womack. Or someone does. But first things first... I gotta find Gracie."

Riley got up from the table and headed for the door. He looked down at the floor. "Shit..." He paused a moment. "Okay, if you want me to go out there with you, I—"

"No. But I appreciate it. Just promise me, Captain asks any questions, you don't know a thing."

Sean and Jenna drove to Nora's after lunch so Sean could check on her, see how she was doing. He turned into the driveway and looked up at the house. "What the hell's she doing?"

Nora had three travel bags out on the top steps in front of the door. She waved her hand at Sean. But not as a greeting but to tell him something.

Jenna lowered the passenger window.

Nora said, "Move your car!"

Sean and Jenna exchanged a glance as Sean shifted into reverse and backed out into the street. They parked and walked up the driveway.

He stopped at the bottom of the stairs and gave

Nora a look. "What are the bags for?"

Nora looked out toward the street as if she didn't hear what he'd said.

"Nora?" He gave Jenna a quick glance, then turned back to Nora. "What are the bags for?"

She still wouldn't look him in the eye. "I'm going back to Maine."

He put his hands on his hips. "You're leaving? Why would you go back to Maine?"

Nora picked up two of the bags and headed for the driveway.

But Sean reached down and took them from her hands. "Nora? Will you tell me what's going on?"

She turned back and grabbed the third bag. She looked at her watch. "I'm going to be late."

"You're leaving? Just like that?" Sean was unable to wrap his mind around a woman leaving when her only daughter was missing.

She shrugged. "You expect me to sit around here? There's not much I can do right now."

Jenna's eyes were wide open as she and Sean exchanged another look. "Mrs. Reed, don't you think it would be better if you waited to go back?"

A gold-colored Crown Victoria drove past the cruiser and turned into Nora's driveway. An older gentleman in a tan suit popped the trunk and stepped out. He left the car running and reached down for Nora's bags, giving Sean and Jenna a nod. "Good afternoon, Officers." He put the bags in the trunk and opened the back door, gestured for Nora to step inside. "Ma'am?"

She shook her head. "I have to lock the front door. Give me a minute." She turned and walked up to her house.

Sean and Jenna stood quietly with the driver.

The driver tried to break the silence. "Nice day, isn't it?"

Sean hadn't thought much about it. Seemed like every other day in Florida at this time of year. He looked at the driver. "When did she call you to set up this ride?"

The man shrugged. "I don't take the calls. I just do the driving. But I believe it was yesterday at some point."

Sean turned and looked at Jenna. "Last minute, don't you think?"

Jenna kept her eyes on him and had a look like she didn't know what he was thinking. "Why's that matter?"

Sean watched Nora come back outside and pull the door closed. She slipped the key in the door and turned the lock, turned the knob and pulled on it a handful of times, making sure it was locked. "Not that it'd make a difference... bastards'll just break my windows again."

She walked out to the car, and the man again opened the rear passenger door. She looked at the grass behind Sean. "Those lawn people do a nice job." She stepped inside. "They're a little expensive, but at least they do what they say they're going to do." She turned and looked at Sean. "Unlike some people..." She pulled the door closed and leaned back in the seat with her eyes fixed on the front of the car.

The man in the tan suit stepped into the front seat and closed the door, backed the car out of the driveway.

Jenna turned to Sean. "Was that some sort of dig at *you*?" she said.

Sean didn't answer but started down the driveway toward the cruiser.

Jenna followed after him and picked up the pace to catch up. "Why'd you ask the driver when she called?"

Sean pulled open the driver's side door but stood outside with one arm rested on top of the hot roof. He looked across at Jenna. "Nora's a planner. I know she's having a harder time with all of this than she'd like to let on. But last minute, like that? To leave again for the rest of the summer?" He turned and watched as the gold Crown Victoria drove past them. "I don't know if there's anything to it. Nora's never been one anyone could figure out."

31

DANNY WOKE UP on the couch. His head pounded. He wiped spit from his chin and sat up straight with his eyes squinted, the bright sun shooting through the cracks in the blinds. He scratched his head. "Carla?"

He walked over to the paintings, still leaned up against the wall, then headed down the hall. He heard voices and pressed his ear up against the bedroom door where the girl was tied up. It was Carla's voice.

He turned the knob but it was locked. "Carla? What the hell's going on in there?" He wiggled the handle with force. "Carla? Open the door..." It hurt to talk, like someone had poured paste down the back of his throat and let it dry.

The door opened and Carla stuck her face in the crack. She had the ski mask down over her face. "We're just talking." She stepped out, pulled the door closed behind her, and walked by Danny. She turned to face him and pulled the mask up onto her head. "How are you feeling?"

He didn't answer. "What the hell's wrong with you?" He grabbed her by the wrist. "You can't be in there talking to her like that... like it's some goddamn slumber party."

She pulled her arm from his grasp and walked out into the room with the paintings. "She's not supposed to be here," she said. "This wasn't part of the plan... kidnap some poor woman who just happened to show up at her mother's house. She hadn't talked to her in over ten years."

"She tell you that?"

Carla nodded. "She followed her father up to New York."

"He's the painter?"

"Who do you think he is? Yes, he's the painter. And with her mother out of town, she thought she'd have a place to stay." She walked into the kitchen, reached into the refrigerator and pulled out a carton of OJ. She poured herself a glass and drank it with her back to Danny. She finished it then turned, her back against the counter.

"What happened to Charles?" Danny said. "Where'd he go?"

"You don't remember?"

Danny stared back at her but didn't really answer. He knew some things went down that he wished maybe hadn't. "He mad?"

Carla took a moment. "He wasn't happy. But he promised me he'd hold up his end of the deal, see if he can still flip the paintings. But he wants more than twenty-five percent. He said a fifty-fifty split, and he'll try to get the original buyer involved again."

"Fifty-fifty? Is he kidding me? There won't be nothing left for the rest of us. A few grand, at best." He stepped toward the window and looked down into the street. "We need to find those other paintings. The ones worth real money."

"They're probably long gone," Carla said. "You didn't ask Jimmy what he knew about them?"

Danny shook his head. "Jimmy wouldn't know *what* was worth *what*. I can't imagine he handpicked the right paintings, went and sold 'em on the streets. He was sitting tight until he could find someone to help him."

"You should've asked him about them before you shot him, Danny."

"He pulled a goddamn gun on me. I told you that." He coughed from deep inside his chest, made a scratching noise from his throat and spit into the sink.

"Maybe you should lay off the booze for a little while, let your head clear till we figure all this out."

He shrugged his shoulders. "What about *you*? Spend your days stoned... wake and bake seven days a week."

Carla waved her hand through the air and walked through the doorway and into the other room. "Weed doesn't make me want to fight and act like an asshole."

Danny walked to the couch where he'd slept, lifted the blanket, and tossed it on the floor. "Where's my .38?"

"I tried to take it from you. You wouldn't let me. Had it in your hands... held it like a doll against your chest." She cracked a slight smile, turned, and lifted the blinds on the window. The sun brightened up the room like someone had flipped a switch.

She walked out to the kitchen, came back in the room with a half-smoked joint in her hand. She lit it and took a hit. "Veronica's pretty upset, you know." Her voice was strained, holding in the smoke.

"You told her?"

Carla blew out the smoke, her eyes wide. "*You* told her. Right before you passed out. It didn't go over well... the way you said it. Like it wasn't a big deal."

"Shit." He pulled the cushions off the couch and tossed them on the floor. "Help me find my gun, will you?"

She took another hit from the joint then walked around the corner into the kitchen. She came back empty handed. "It's got to be here somewhere, hon."

He had his hands on his hips, shaking his head. He took a deep breath and exhaled air through his tightened lips. He walked into the kitchen and looked out the window and into the parking lot. "There a car I can use?"

Carla turned in the doorway to face him. "Just the Chevy. But I already told Veronica not to drive it. Jimmy's sister might've told the cops what you were driving."

He turned from the window. "Where are the keys?"

Carla didn't answer but her eyes went to the table. "You shouldn't go out there now. Probably best you lay low for a few days."

He followed Carla's eyes and reached for the keys, turned, and headed for the door. He pulled it open and held his hand on the knob. "I gotta go see Maggie, make sure she didn't say nothin' to the cops."

"Jimmy's sister? You can't, Danny. She's the one who called the cops. You killed her brother."

He shook his head. "You don't know Maggie. And the way Jimmy talks, she might know what he did with those other paintings. Shit, she might even have 'em hidden somewhere in her house. Maybe that'd be enough, she'd keep her mouth shut." He opened the door and stepped outside.

Carla grabbed him by the arm. "If you find the other paintings, do you promise we're gonna let Gracie go?"

He stared back at her and pulled his arm from her grasp, then reached behind for the back of his pants and patted his pockets. "Shit," he said. "My goddamn gun." He looked back into the apartment. "See if you can find it while I'm gone."

"You're going out there without a gun? Don't you think you should—"

"Got a Glock out under the seat in the truck... the one Jimmy almost shot me with."

32

SEAN STOOD OUTSIDE Maggie's house and rang the doorbell. It was quiet inside... no crying baby. No TV. He waited a few moments then knocked. "Maggie? You in there?" He tried to turn the knob, but it was locked. He looked toward the driveway but didn't know if she even had a car other than the Lincoln under the carport with the two flat tires.

He walked back out to the Explorer, leaned over and reached under the front seat. He came out with his SIG Sauer, undid his belt and ran it through the holster as he walked up the driveway. He had his eyes on the Lincoln.

He was about to turn to Maggie's door but instead walked past the Lincoln, looked toward the side door under the carport but kept going. He stopped when he saw a Chevy S-10 pickup parked in the tall grass behind the house. The grass was matted down from the tires. Sean could see the fresh tracks where the truck drove in a circle in front of a rusted metal shed. The truck faced the road and hadn't been there long.

Sean unsnapped the holster. He removed his SIG Sauer and held it with both hands toward the ground. He moved closer to the truck and looked around the yard. He stood just outside the driver's side and raised his gun with his head in a position to look inside.

The truck was empty.

He looked behind it toward the shed, then started for the back door of the house. He stepped across the concrete patio and up two steps, reached for the doorknob, but the door opened without a turn. He used his foot and pushed it farther. He stepped inside the kitchen, and his eyes went to shattered glass on the linoleum floor.

He tried to step over it, but his boot crunched down on a piece of glass. He went through the kitchen and into the room with the TV, then turned down the short hallway where he saw the picture of Maggie and her brother with Danny Womack. He was light with each step and turned into the bathroom. With his gun raised in one hand pointed into the shower, he reached for the curtain and ripped it open.

There were a couple of shampoo bottles, a bar of soap, and a baby's tub with toys floating in white, soapy water.

He stepped out of the bathroom and turned right. Behind him was another door. He turned and reached for the knob, swung open the door and stepped in with his gun raised.

The room with two walls painted pink had an empty crib in the corner but not much else. There were pictures of ducks and bunnies on a border along the top of one of two painted walls. With his gun raised, he opened a bifold closet door. But other than a few metal hangers on a wooden pole, there was nothing inside it.

Sean stepped across the hall and into the other bedroom. He tried to ease his breathing. The adrenaline made his heart pound in his chest. He heard a noise coming from the other side of the door. Without another thought he lifted his boot and kicked it open.

Maggie's little girl, April, smiled up at him from a white bassinet. Her eyes were wide open, and she stretched out her arms toward him.

In a hushed voice, he said, "Where's your mommy?" He looked around the room, and knew the first thing he had to do was to get the baby out of there. He tucked his SIG Sauer into his holster and pulled out his phone. He sent Jenna a text:

Call Lake City PD... 9-1-1. I'm at Maggie Stanish's house.

An engine turned over outside the bedroom

window. Sean pulled his gun again and looked down at April. "Don't go anywhere." He ran from the bedroom and down the hall, ripped open the back door and ran for the Chevy S-10 with his gun raised in front of him. "Stop!"

Maggie was in the driver's seat. And the man he knew, without a doubt, to be Danny Womack was in the passenger seat with a gun pointed at Maggie's head.

She didn't turn to look at Sean. The sun reflected off the passenger-side window, but he could see the tears coming down Maggie's cheek.

Danny glanced at Sean and smiled. The window went down a handful of inches and Danny lifted himself so his mouth was near the window. "Take another step toward this truck, Officer... her blood'll be on your hands."

Sean kept the gun raised. "Let her go, Danny. Her baby needs her. Please."

Danny, again, got his mouth up near the opening at the top of the window. "I'm warning you. Put your gun down. Or she dies." He slid closer to Maggie and wrapped his arm around her shoulder. He brought her head down in a headlock and pressed the gun into her skull.

Sean had a pretty good feeling the gun in Danny's hand was the Glock Jimmy took from Nora's house.

"Let her go, Danny. The cops are on their way. You're not going to get away with any of this." He heard Danny yell and tell her to put the goddamn car in drive.

Maggie reached for the shifter on the steering wheel. The transmission clanked when she pulled it down and the truck moved forward.

Sean wanted to take a shot. If he'd had his Glock, he would have. But it'd been a while since he shot his SIG Sauer... years since he took it to the range. And he wasn't going to risk Maggie's life.

Sirens were off in the distance but grew louder.

Maggie pulled past the Lincoln into the driveway, and Danny stuck the Glock out the window.

Danny took a shot at him, and Sean dove behind the house. He stayed low and crouched behind the Lincoln and watched the truck pick up speed and head toward the road.

The truck turned, and Sean thought he had a clear shot at Danny but brought his gun down before he pulled the trigger.

Danny fired another shot. The window on the Lincoln exploded.

Sean ran down the driveway and jumped into his Explorer just as Lake City Police vehicles turned onto the road in front of Maggie's house.

An officer jumped from the car's passenger side and raised his gun, had it pointed on Sean. "Get out of the car!"

Sean placed his gun down on the dash and raised both hands so the officer could see he wasn't armed.

"I'm an officer with the Jacksonville Sheriff's Office."

The officer kept his gun on Sean. "Step out of the car."

Sean got out and turned his waist so the officer could see the badge clipped to his belt. He nodded in the direction Danny and Maggie had headed. "They went that way. A black Chevy S-10. Man's name is Danny Womack." He turned toward the house. "There's a baby girl inside. Her name's April. Danny Womack has her mother."

33

DANNY TOOK OVER behind the wheel of the S-10. The truck cab rattled the faster he tried to get it to go. He turned off 247 and headed east on 240. His eyes shifted from the rearview mirror to the highway ahead of them. He wondered if he'd have to ditch the truck, guessing there could be a roadblock along the way.

He didn't have much choice but to keep heading north, get the hell out of Florida, and at least into Georgia. He could hide at his cousin's place out in Folkston.

It'd been a while since they talked.

Maggie pleaded with him. *"Please, Danny.* April needs me. Please. Don't kill me, Danny. I swear I won't tell anyone a thing."

He gave her a quick glance, caught her eyes down on the gun under his hand, rested on the seat. "Don't you go comin' up with some stupid idea,

Maggie."

"I'm not coming up with anything. I just... I just don't want you to shoot me."

Danny let out a slight laugh and shook his head, his eyes ahead on the road. He knew he had to ditch the truck and find some other wheels, but there wasn't much around. After another couple of miles, he saw a cross on the grass in front of a church. He cut the wheel hard and turned into the parking lot of the Belmont Christian Church. The tires skidded and he straightened out the wheel, drove straight then around to the back of the building. He pulled up next to a faded blue van with a lot of windows and more than just a few rows of seats. It almost looked like a bus, but smaller. There was rust on the lower side of the van, and the paint on the hood was a different shade of blue.

He held the Glock on Maggie and grabbed her by the arm, pulled her toward him and out the driver's side.

She looked around. "What are we doing here? What are you going to do?"

He held her by the arm and his fingers dug into her skin. "If I was going to kill you, church'd sure be the best place to do it. I mean, for your sake... good Christian girl like you." He pulled her along behind him and glanced at her over his shoulder, that crooked, devilish smile on his face. He shook his head. "I ain't gonna hurt you, Maggie. I told you that already. Just... just don't do anything stupid. You got it?" He pulled her along and walked to the back door of the building.

There weren't any windows to look inside. He knocked on the heavy steel door, then noticed a button he guessed was a doorbell. He pressed it and held his finger down, heard the buzz on the other side.

The door opened, and a big man, with a thick neck and body almost as wide as the door's opening, stood on the other side. "Can I help you?"

Danny nodded. "Yeah, I think you can." He pointed with his thumb over his shoulder." You can give me the keys to that van."

The man looked beyond Danny and Maggie toward the Chevy parked next to the faded blue van. He shook his head then tried to pull the door closed. But Danny stuck his foot in the way and kept it from closing.

The man held his hand on the door's knob, kept pressure on Danny's foot, and looked out at them through the opening. "I'm not going to give you the keys to that van. It's for the kids... we use it for our trips."

Danny cracked a crooked smile. "Who drives it, Chester the Molester?" He turned and looked at Maggie, thinking she'd laugh. But she didn't. He turned back to the man and gave him a nod with his chin. "That you? You drive the little church boys around, take them out to the mountain?" He pulled the Glock from his pants and slid his arm through the opening, pushed the muzzle into the man's cheek. "Is that your name? Chester?"

Beads of sweat covered the man's forehead. "It's Gary."

Danny moved his head back and forth, tried to look past the man's big head and into the building. "How many boys you got hiding back there, Chester?"

Gary tried to shake his head but didn't move much with the muzzle jammed into his fat cheeks. His eyes were down on the gun. "There's nobody else here. It's just me." He looked Danny in the eye. "Please. Don't shoot me. I'll give you the keys."

Danny kept the gun on the man's face and opened the door, pointed it at his back when the man turned. "Let's go... go get 'em, Chester." He kept the gun pointed at the man's back and dragged Maggie by the arm. They walked down a hall and turned into a small office no bigger than a broom closet. A desk and a chair faced the doorway.

The man sat down behind the desk and leaned back so he could pull open the drawer in front of his big stomach. "I'm not sure what I did with them." He gave Danny a look, then reached down into a drawer to the side. His head practically disappeared behind the desk, then he came up and fired a gun of his own, missed Danny by a good two feet... put a hole in the wall, next to the framed picture of Jesus.

Danny fired off two quick shots with the Glock, emptied a couple of .40s into the man. One in the face. One clipped his ear. Danny fired another, got him in the chest.

The man stared back at them and slouched in the chair. His bloody face dropped and smashed on top of the desk.

Maggie screamed and started to cry.

Danny walked around the desk and used his foot to push him off the chair and out of the way. The man's body fell from the chair and plopped on the floor. Danny reached inside the middle drawer and grabbed a ring of keys then turned the gun to Maggie. "Hopefully it's one of these." He nodded toward the door. "Let's go."

Danny walked behind her with the gun pointed at her back. They walked out to the van and Maggie cried. "You can't just go around killing people like that, Danny. That poor man was—"

"Oh, shut the hell up, will you?" He grabbed her by the arm and tucked the Glock in the back of his pants. He looked at the keys in his hand and picked out the one that looked like it'd go with the van, opened the driver's side and shoved Maggie inside. He pushed her over to the passenger side and stepped in behind her.

He tried the same key in the ignition but it didn't fit. "Shit." He tried three more before he found the right one, slid the key in and turned it. But the van didn't start. "Goddammit," he said. He tried it again, this time pumped the gas pedal. The engine turned over. He looked in the rearview, and white smoke filled the parking lot behind them. He put his hand on the back of Maggie's seat under her blonde hair and backed out of the parking space.

"Where are you taking me?" she said. "My baby..."

"Cops are there." He straightened out the wheel and drove for the exit. "I'm sure they'll take good care of her. Find her a nice family'll raise her right." He laughed.

"A good family? What are you..." Maggie burst out crying. "You can't do this, Danny. Please, just let me go. I swear, as God is my judge, I won't tell no one you shot Jimmy." She turned and looked at the church. "Or that poor innocent man..."

Danny turned the corner on 240. "We're going to Georgia." He turned to Maggie. "You gonna tell me what Jimmy did with those paintings, or you gonna keep playing dumb?"

"I told you, Danny. I have no idea."

He gave her a look, then shifted his eyes to the rearview. The white smoke poured from the back of the van. "Jimmy could never keep that fat mouth of his shut. I don't believe he didn't tell you what he had back behind your house. Or that you didn't ask."

Maggie stared back at him. "We hardly talked while he was there. That's the truth."

Danny tried to keep the van under the speed limit, but it was hard... he was anxious to get over the state line. And they still had a few miles to go before they'd hit 90.

The two were both quiet for the next few miles.

Danny looked at Maggie, her eyes out the passenger window. Her head was tilted a bit to the side. "You awake?" he said, slapped her leg with the back of his hand.

She lifted her head from the window. She didn't answer, turned back and looked the other way.

"It was self-defense, you know. Jimmy pulled on me." He looked down at the gun in his hand between them. "This was the gun, in fact. Pretty sure he stole it from that cop, was at your house."

Danny was trying to be cool now, thought about turning on the radio but didn't mind the quiet, either. He looked down at Maggie's legs coming out of her shorts. "Jimmy was like a brother to me. You know that. He didn't give me a choice, Maggie."

She turned from the window, tears on her face. "I didn't tell them it was you. I didn't say a word. I wasn't going to... I won't. I promise you that, Danny. You gotta believe me... just let me go. I'll get out here, hitchhike my way home."

He kept his eyes straight ahead, acted as if he hadn't heard a word.

"Danny?" she said. "Please? My little girl..."

He turned and gave her a look. "If you didn't tell

the sheriff's office, then how come that officer was —"

"I didn't say a word. I swear. I told him he'd need a warrant to come in. But he came in anyway."

Danny reached down and turned on the van's lights. His voice calm, he said, "You mean it? You didn't tell them it was me?"

"No. I didn't say nothin'."

He turned onto 90. "Why not?"

"Why not *what*?"

"Why didn't you tell them?"

She took a moment before she answered and stared at Danny from the side. "Because I don't want my baby growin' up like *I* did... with her daddy stuck in prison."

34

SEAN HEARD CAPTAIN Ward yell for him as soon as he walked into the station. Jenna walked next to him, and the two walked down the hall together, but she turned off before they got to Ward's office door. She wished him luck and headed in the other direction.

Sean wasn't some rookie cop barely over drinking age, wearing a badge. So walking into Ward's office wasn't what it used to be, a kid screwing up working the streets. His superiors were more intimidating back then. And twice his age at the time.

This time it was different.

Captain Ward had his eyes down on a piece of paper he held in his hands, his glasses on the edge of his nose. He looked up at Sean, flipped the paper into the manila folder and closed it. He leaned back in his chair and pulled off his glasses.

Sean stood at attention, his chest out. "Sir?"

The captain nodded at the two chairs in front of Sean. "Close the door and take a seat." He leaned forward on the desk, his eyes somewhat squinted as Sean turned and looked at him from the door.

Sean sat down and silence filled the office. He stared back at the captain and repeated what he'd already said. "Sir?"

"I just got off the phone with Chief Rolfes out at Lake City PD. Would you like to guess who he's pointing his finger at? Letting a murder suspect flee... the victim's sister missing?"

Sean nodded. "That would be me, sir."

"No." Captain Ward shook his head and pointed his thick finger toward his chest. "Chief Rolfes is blaming *me*." He pushed the folder off to the side of his desk and folded his hands in front of him. "You know why? Because he believes I allowed one of my officers to get involved in a crime that took place outside of our jurisdiction. He made it clear he would've asked me if he wanted our help." He took a deep breath and shook his head. "Rolfes'd have to be down to his last man before he'd ask me for help." He ran his hand over the stubble on top of his shaved head. "He said it's an officer under my command who went rogue, off duty, and stepped in shit while they were in the middle of an investigation he said is now in worse shape than when they started."

"Sir, I—"

"You've not only given our division a black eye, but you've given the entire Jacksonville Sheriff's Office bad press we simply don't need right now. It's all over the news." He picked up the paper in front of him, slipped his glasses back onto his face. He read, "Former training officer with the JSO's training academy visits the sister of a homicide victim. Leads to her kidnapping." He looked over his glasses at Sean. "Baby girl left behind, turned over to Lake City DCF." He took off his glasses and laid them down on top of the paper. "Does that sound like good press to you?"

Sean shook his head.

"Now, I know your cousin's involved in this. And we're doing all we can to find her. So it's personal for you. I understand that. But you can't break the law, Sean. You can't go after a man who—"

"I know I was wrong. But he knows where Gracie is. All I was doing was looking for answers."

"We have procedures for a reason. We have relationships with departments all around Northeast Florida. You crossed the line. I think you know that." The captain pulled open his drawer and slid another piece of paper across the desk. "I'm sorry, Sean, but you leave me with no choice." He paused a moment, looked directly at Sean across the desk. "You're suspended until further notice."

Sean stared back at the captain, then leaned forward in the chair, his elbows rested on his knees.

He closed his eyes then looked down at the floor for a few moments before he lifted his head again. "But sir, I—"

"It's out of my hands. I know you understand. And believe me, I did what I could." He looked at the window between his office and the hallway. "You're a good cop. And I was glad to have you in my division." He scratched the side of his head. "It may only be a few days. A week, at most."

"So what is this... just a PR move?"

Captain Ward shook his head. "Come on, Sean. You know better than that. If anyone knows how it works, it's you." He stood up from his desk and cracked a slight smile. "Now, maybe you'll remember it's a lot easier to teach the rules than to follow them."

Sean drove by Nora's house and pulled behind Gracie's old BMW. He walked up and looked inside the car, nothing but a mess with empty soda cans and clothes tossed all over the seats.

He thought about Gracie and how he barely knew her. Never really did other than when they were little. When she left for New York, he was the last to know. He never even had her number or email address or cared to ask for it. He would've felt guilty contacting her, the way she left Nora all alone.

He let himself inside the house with the key Nora'd given him a long time ago. The old house was dark with a damp and musty smell. She'd turned the air-conditioning off while she was gone, to save on electricity. With the humidity so high in the summer months, she was lucky the hardwoods weren't twisted.

Sean walked over the area on the floor where Jimmy Stanish had knocked him out and took his gun. He looked at the couch where Nora was tied up, then walked past the baby grand and stepped into the kitchen. He opened the refrigerator, hoping there might be something to drink. But it was empty. He looked around for Gracie's keys but didn't see them hanging on the hook. He thought maybe they were held in evidence... and wished he'd checked, but he hadn't thought of it until then.

He headed back outside to Gracie's Beemer and pressed his face up against the hot glass on the driver's side, his hands up on either side of his face to block the glare from the sun. What a mess.

He looked around the ground and crouched down to pick up a rock from the edge of the driveway. He straightened up and looked around at the neighbors' houses. You couldn't see much of anything. With one flick, he tossed the rock against the car window and the glass shattered into hundreds of little pieces.

He reached his hand through the opening and unlocked the door from the inside, then opened it.

He leaned inside over the seat, careful not to rest his hand in the glass, then reached for the center console. There was no top, and it was stuffed with enough paper to make a whole book. He pulled it all out, walked around to the hood of the car and dumped it all on top. He shuffled through the papers but didn't find much of anything, stepped back to the car and reached over to the glove box. He reached inside and pulled out the owner's manual and an envelope. He looked inside it and found a key.

He walked back to the hood with the key in his hand and looked through the papers. There were receipts, a parking ticket, and a couple of overdue bills. Some of the receipts were for a store called Do It Again. Whatever that was. He opened a folded piece of paper, a receipt for a storage unit at a place called U-Store-It. The address in the top corner was for a place up in Kingsland, just over the line in Georgia.

35

"IT WAS ON the news," Carla said. "They know who you are... what you look like. And it's only a matter of time before they track the rest of us down, show up at my door looking for you."

Danny stood alone in his cousin Wayne's kitchen. He had the phone up to his ear, listening to Carla go on and on. "Are you done?" he said. "I don't need to be spoken to like you're my mother. Not right now. And, well, it's not like I go around telling everyone about you. I don't mean that in a bad way, but... I'm just saying, stop worrying they'll be able to connect you to any of this."

Carla said, "Well, you're kidding yourself if you think nobody'll be able to point a finger at me, tell the cops the man going in and out of my apartment looks an awful lot like the one they saw on TV."

Danny rolled his eyes and held his hair back on his head. "Carla, will you just shut up for one second?

You need to do me a favor."

"I don't know," she said. "I might have to just get out of here before the cops—"

"Just listen. I need you to bring the girl up here... to my cousin Wayne's place."

"But what am I supposed to drive?"

He looked out through the front window. "Shit. I don't know. You'll have to call Curtis. Didn't he get another car yet? You'll need two of you anyway... one to keep an eye on her, make sure she don't run off."

"I could call Veronica, see if she can—"

"Not a good idea. I don't even want her to know where I am... sure she's still steamed about what happened to Jimmy."

The two were quiet for a moment.

Carla said, "So why'd you take Jimmy's sister with you?"

"How'd you hear that?"

"I told you. It's all over the news. They're looking for you. That's what I'm telling you. I don't know where your cousin lives, but wherever it is, I'm not sure it's far enough."

"All right. Hold your titties, will you? Let me think." Danny took a moment and stared out toward the dirt driveway where he'd parked the van. "You gotta just get her up here. Whatever you gotta do. So grab a pen, write this down. It's the only way I'll get that cop off my ass."

Carla was quiet.

"Carla?"

She took a moment before she spoke. "Danny, I need to tell you something."

Danny cocked his head back. "Christ, Carla. I'm trying to figure out what the hell to do here. You just keep going on and on about—"

Carla said, "She knows where the paintings are."

Danny heard Carla. Loud and clear. But he asked anyway. "What the hell did you just say?"

"Gracie knows where the paintings are. There are three of them. And they're worth a lot of money. More than all the others together."

Danny stuck his tongue inside his cheek and walked to the front door, looked through the screen toward Wayne seated on a picnic table in the tall grass out front. He had a 12 gauge rested across his lap.

Maggie was across from him.

Danny turned back from the door. "Carla, what the hell are you talking about?"

"She said if we let her go, she'll tell me where they are. She said I can have 'em, do whatever I want. As long as I let her live."

Danny pulled open the fridge, took out a can of beer and cracked the top with one hand. He took a swig and snarled his lip, let out a big burp. "Put her on the phone."

"No. You can't say anything to her about it. She

told me not to tell anyone else... she'd only make the deal with me."

"Then let me just talk to her. I won't say anything... just make sure she's—"

"Let me call Curtis. We'll bring her up to you."

"*Now* you want to bring her up here?" He narrowed his eyes and threw back the rest of the beer. "What the hell's going on here, Carla?"

She kept her voice low and whispered into the phone. "Danny, she trusts me. I don't want to blow it. Not if she's gonna point us toward those paintings."

"Jesus, Carla. Put her on the goddamn phone!"

The line went quiet. After a couple of moments, she said, "Hang on." The sound on the other end was muffled, like Carla's hand was over the mouthpiece. He tried to listen to the voices in the background but couldn't make out what they were saying.

Then the line went quiet.

Danny held the phone away from his face and yelled into it, like it was alive. "Carla! Pick up the goddamn phone!" He pressed it against his ear. "You there?"

"Jesus, Danny. And you're telling *me* to relax? Listen, give me some time. I have to find a car. And I don't even know where Folkston is, but I'm guessing it'll be at least a couple hours."

"We don't have a couple of hours."

She said, "I'll do whatever I can," then ended the call.

Danny stared at the phone, shaking his head. He pulled open the refrigerator and grabbed the three beers left in the six-pack, held it by the plastic rings with one finger and walked outside to the picnic table.

Maggie had a smile on her face, Wayne saying something but stopped when Danny walked over and placed two cans on the table. He cracked the third open for himself and threw his head back, took a good swig. "What the hell's going on out here?" He looked at Maggie. "I didn't bring you here to flirt with my cousin."

Wayne gave him a look. "Relax, Danny. We're just talkin'."

He pulled out the Glock and pointed it at Wayne. "Next person who tells me to relax is going to get one of these." He put his foot up on the bench of the picnic table and looked away, shaking his head, leaned down with his forearms rested on his thigh. The gun hung loose in his hand. He sipped his beer and glanced at Maggie. He reached for the two beers and pulled one from the plastic ring, cracked the top, and handed it to her. "Here. Have a drink, will you?"

She looked down at the beer in his hand and shook her head. "I'm worried about April, Danny. My baby girl." She looked down toward the ground, then raised her eyes back up to him. "*Your* little girl."

Wayne had just sipped his beer and spit it out all over Maggie when what she'd just said came out of her mouth. "What did you just say?" He looked back and forth from Danny to Maggie. "Wait a minute... you mean... you and Danny have a baby?"

Danny pushed him. "Shut up, Wayne. That's not what she meant." He narrowed his eyes with a slight tilt to his head and looked down at her. "Why would you say something stupid like that? You think you can fool me... hope I'll just let you go?"

Maggie took the beer Danny'd put down on the picnic table and took a sip. "I haven't been with nobody else, Danny. Not in a long time." She looked him straight in the eye. "April is your baby girl."

36

MAC WAS ALREADY seated at a table at the back of Jazzy Café when Sean walked in the door, plainclothed, with sunglasses over his eyes. He pulled the glasses from his face and hung them on the collar of his T-shirt, walked up to Mac and pulled out a chair.

Mac held a coffee in his hand and looked across at Sean. "You all right? You look like shit."

Sean tried to force a smile. "Thanks. Wish I could say the same about you... but you look better than you have in ten years."

Mac had a multicolored, button-down shirt with short sleeves. Something you'd wear bowling... in Hawaii. "That's how it's supposed to work," he said. "Maybe you should give it a try."

"Retirement?" Sean looked at the young woman behind the counter.

Mac said, "You have to admit... it's a different world out there. A lot different from what it was when you and I were first out on the streets."

Sean got up from his seat, had little interest in the conversation Mac seemed to have in mind. "Let me grab a coffee." He nodded toward Mac's cup. "You need another one?"

Mac leaned his cup and looked inside. He shook his head. "This is my second one."

Sean ordered a black coffee from the girl behind the counter, grabbed his coffee and sat back down at the table with Mac.

Mac said, "I'm sorry. I know this hasn't been easy on you. You could've never expected any of this."

Sean paused a moment. "Not in a million years." He sipped his coffee and leaned forward on the table, both hands wrapped around the paper cup. "I'd be better off a vigilante. I forgot how much red tape there was... keeps you from doing your job." He looked down into his cup. "I can't even get any information. Nobody'll talk to me. Not even Jenna. Who knows what he did with Gracie, and now he's got Jimmy's sister." Sean's eyes went to the door as a man walked in with an obvious limp.

The man headed for the counter.

Mac turned and looked. "You know him?"

Sean shook his head.

They both watched the man turn from the counter with a cup in his hand. He started past their table, then stopped. He looked Sean in the eye. "Any chance you're with the Jacksonville Sheriff's Office?"

Sean hesitated a moment before he answered. He straightened out in his seat but didn't answer. "Is there something I can help you with?"

"You look like the officer who was at Raceway, out at Murray Hill. I was assaulted. Some crazy bastard came after me in the parking lot." He looked down at his leg. "Smashed my leg in my car door. You look like the officer who showed up... with a very attractive female officer I wouldn't mind running into again." He smirked.

Sean nodded. "I thought I recognized you." He looked down. "How's the leg?"

The man nodded. "Somehow, it didn't break. But it's a mess." He sipped his coffee. "The thing is, I actually called the sheriff's office a couple of times, hoping to talk to you."

Sean said. "I'm sorry, but this is the first I've heard of it. I never got the message. But I'm actually off duty now, so—"

"I didn't remember your name so I didn't know who to ask for. But, listen, I called because the man who assaulted me... I actually saw him on the news. I know they're looking for him. He's the one who kidnapped that young woman, the mother, out there in Lake City. Shot a man, too, from what I heard."

Sean and Mac exchanged a look.

Sean looked up at the man. "What's your name again?"

"Craig. Craig Warburton."

Sean squinted his eyes, quiet for a moment. He looked across the table at Mac. "That young woman working behind the counter..."

Mac said, "Veronica Hobson. She's Chief Hobson's daughter. I've been in there for lunch a couple times since then... haven't seen her."

The man said, "The big girl, right?" He nodded. "She was this guy's friend. His name is Danny or something."

"Danny Womack," Sean said.

The man nodded again. "Yeah. That's it. Well, that big girl from the gas station, she worked behind the counter with the fried chicken. She's the one who, well... I might've said some things I shouldn't have. But I know he was friends with her. He made a comment about it when he slammed my leg in the car door."

Sean looked at Mac. "We talked to her. In fact, she quit right after. Or she might've gotten fired... I didn't get involved in any of the BS. But she swore to me she had no idea who he was."

Mac shrugged. "She was lying."

Sean looked up at the man, hair slicked back... had a way about him. You could see why someone might want to give him a good shove. "Okay, well... thank you for bringing it to my attention."

The man looked back and forth between Sean and Mac. "That's it?"

Mac stood from his seat, towered over the man by

a good six inches. "He told you he's off duty. And we're trying to enjoy our coffee. If you don't mind?" Mac crossed his arms over his chest.

The man stepped back, raised both hands, still holding his coffee. He turned and headed for the door, looked back at Sean and Mac through the glass and shook his head as he disappeared into the parking lot.

Mac sat back down at the table and looked into his empty cup. "I remember you told me when it happened. You thought that would be the most excitement you'd see over there."

Sean nodded, leaned back in his chair, and thought for a moment. "I need to find Veronica Hobson."

Mac started to nod but stopped. "You gotta be careful, Sean. You're suspended. Word gets around you're out doing your own rogue investigation..."

"It's my cousin, Mac. They can't expect me to just sit back." He took a deep breath and leaned forward on the table. "I'm not sure I care what happens with my job. Not right now. I need to find Gracie. And to be honest, I'm responsible for what happened to Maggie Stanish. Anything happens to either of them..."

"But you won't be much use if they throw you behind bars for working while under suspension. That's just the way it works, Sean. I think you know that."

Sean shook his head. "Don't worry, I'm not going

to jail." He got up from the table and threw the coffee he'd barely touched in the garbage.

They both headed for the door.

Sean put his hand out. "Mind if I use your phone?"

Mac looked down at the one Sean had in his hand. "Yours no good?"

"I gotta call Jenna. She won't take my call if she's at the station and knows it's me."

Mac scratched his head, then handed Sean his phone as they walked out into the parking lot.

Sean looked at his phone for her number, then dialed Mac's phone.

Jenna answered on the first ring.

"Jenna. It's me. Don't hang up."

"I can't talk."

"Just listen. I need a favor."

She was quiet for a moment. "Ward warned me already, if I—"

"Just listen. We need to find a young woman, name's Veronica Hobson."

"Isn't she the one, works at Raceway?"

"Yes, that's her. Can you do a lookup? She might know where Danny Womack is hiding."

37

DANNY TURNED FROM the sink and pulled the Glock from his pants. He walked to the door and looked out through the screen as a full-sized Chevy Suburban pulled into the driveway. He stepped out and walked through the tall grass, watched Curtis turn the wheel and park next to the van. Danny pulled the back passenger door open without a word. He looked in at Gracie with the dark pillow case over her head, reached in and grabbed her by the arm. He pulled her down from the Suburban.

Gracie's hands were tied behind her back. "Ouch," she said. "Careful with those claws."

Danny looked at the passenger door as it opened, watched Carla step down from the passenger side. He held Gracie by the arm with one hand, reached for Carla with the other and grabbed her by the back of her head. She leaned her head back and Danny gave her a long kiss, then pushed her away.

Danny pulled his phone from his pocket, then turned to Curtis stepping around the front of the Suburban. "*Now* you get the big vehicle? Where was this when we needed it?"

Curtis shrugged. "Just got lucky. Grabbed it from a mom, out watching her kids at a soccer field."

Danny started to pull Gracie, then stopped and looked back inside the Suburban. "Where's Veronica?"

Carla said, "You told me not to take her out here."

Danny stared at her for a moment, then nodded. "Right." He pulled the hood off of Gracie's head. "You already know our names... no sense you wear this thing any longer."

Gracie squinted and gave her head a slight shake, squeezed her eyes closed, then looked around. She stared at Carla for a moment before Danny tugged at her arm and pulled her toward the house. He stopped and got a good look at her. She was attractive. Not much younger than Carla, he thought. But just as good looking. He stared at a tattoo on her neck. With a nod, he said, "What's that?"

"What's what?" she said.

"Those lines on your neck?"

"Taurus."

"The car?"

She stared back at him, made a face. "The constellation. Got it for a friend of mine I met in Bedford Hills."

"Bedford Hills?"

"It's a women's prison, in Upstate New York."

"No shit, huh?" Danny nodded, cracked a slight smile, then turned to Curtis. "You hear that?" He pulled Gracie across the grass and up the stairs. He let the door slam as Carla came up behind him and reached for the handle.

Wayne was inside and leaned against the counter with a can of beer in his hand, one arm folded across his chest. He looked at Gracie, then past Danny at Carla as she walked in the door. "Jesus, Danny... how many people you got coming here?"

Danny turned, glanced over his shoulder. "That's Carla. He pulled Gracie by her arm. "This is Gracie." He looked around the kitchen. "Where the hell's Maggie?"

"She went to lay down, back there in my bedroom."

Danny let go of Gracie's arm, his eyebrows wrinkled over his eyes. "Why the hell aren't you in there watching her?" He grabbed the 12 gauge Wayne had leaned up against the counter next to him, walked through the doorway, and down the hall to Wayne's bedroom. He tried to turn the knob, but it was locked. He smacked the door with his palm flat. "Maggie? Open the goddamn door." He pounded, this time with a closed fist. "Maggie? You awake in there? Open the door, before I kick it down."

Wayne and Curtis walked up behind him.

Danny turned to Wayne, put out his hand. "Where's the key?"

Wayne shrugged. "What key?"

Danny shook his head, and without another word he threw his shoulder into the door. It splintered near the knob and crashed open and smashed against the wall on the other side. His eyes went to the bed, then to the sheets and the checked spread bunched up on the floor. He ran across the room to an open window, leaned and looked outside. His eyes went toward the woods behind the house. "Shit!" He turned to the room, brushed past Wayne, and punched the wall as he headed back to the kitchen. He had the 12 gauge in his hand and turned to Wayne, directly behind him.

"I'm sorry, Danny. I didn't think—"

"Jesus Christ, Wayne. You didn't think what? If I didn't want you to watch her I wouldn't have asked you to. You understand?" He looked out through the screen on the front door.

Wayne said, "I told you I didn't want nothin' to do with this shit, Danny."

Curtis walked in the front door, and Danny handed him the 12 gauge. "Maggie's gone. Go see if she's hiding somewhere out there. She don't know these woods... can't imagine she'd go running in there, no idea where she's going." He grabbed Gracie and pulled her out the front door, across the tall grass toward the picnic table. He shoved her down into the seat and pulled the Glock from his pants. "Don't you go getting any ideas to run off like that." He put his foot up on the bench, just a few inches from Gracie's leg.

Curtis turned and yelled from the corner of the house, just before the woods. "Where am I supposed to look?"

Danny scratched his head and looked back at Curtis but didn't answer. He turned to the doorway, caught Carla out of the corner of his eye, then turned back to Gracie. "This man I used to know, Jerry Russo, he used to say don't ever have a plan B. You know why?"

Gracie looked at him and gave a slight shake of her head.

"Because then it's too easy to fall back on your plan B when things start to get a little hairy." He looked into the woods. "But I'm afraid I don't have much of a choice. Because your cousin the cop seems to care enough about you, he'll do what I say... knows I could kill you if he doesn't let me walk out of here." He nodded toward Carla. "Me and her, we're going to get out of here. Somewhere we'll never be found for the rest of our lives. But I can't get out of here with what I got in my pocket, and —"

"You're wrong if you think my cousin cares what happens to me. If he has to make a choice between saving me and killing you..." She didn't finish, turned and glanced at Carla, then stood up from the picnic table.

Danny grabbed Gracie by the arm. "Sit down!" He took his foot off the bench of the picnic table and walked around the other side. "So you gonna tell me where the rest of your daddy's paintings are?"

Gracie glanced at Carla. "I thought you weren't going to tell him?"

Carla shrugged. "I'm sorry, sweetie."

Gracie turned to Danny. "I tell you... you'll let me live?"

He thought for a moment, his eyes narrowed. He hesitated before he spoke. "How would I know you're not just going to set me up?"

She shook her head. "How would I do that? Mental telepathy?" She huffed out a slight laugh. "I haven't spoken to a soul since you abducted me."

"So why'd you take them?" he said.

"The paintings?" She shrugged. "My mother was going to burn them." She looked down toward the ground for a moment before she lifted her eyes back to Danny. "So what's your plan B?"

He shook his head. "I changed my mind. There won't be a plan B. Jerry was right." He turned to Carla. "You talk to Charles?"

"Not yet."

"Well then, what are you waiting for?" He shook his head and rolled his eyes.

Gracie said, "Who's Charles? Is he the one you had back at your apartment? Danny was too drunk to close the deal?" She laughed.

Danny hadn't said more than two words to her the whole time until they took her up to his cousin's house. And he couldn't help but wonder about her. She had a mouth, said whatever she wanted to even though he was the one with the gun. Like she wasn't afraid. "You hear everything we said?"

She didn't answer. "You don't need to call Charles. I already have people lined up who want to buy my father's work. I'll cut you in on the deal as long as we agree you'll let me go."

Danny didn't like the way the ball'd somehow ended up in her court. But he didn't have much choice, other than to keep her hostage, use her to keep the cop out of his hair. He pulled his phone from his pocket and looked at the time. "Maggie makes it out of those woods and gets to a phone, cops'll be out here in no time." He looked Gracie in the eye, put his hand on her thigh. "So where are they?"

"The paintings?"

Danny made a face, cocked his head back a bit. "What the hell else would I be talking about?" He turned and stepped away from the table, ran his hand through his hair. "Jesus Christ..."

"There's one problem," Gracie said.

He turned to her, his hands on his hips. "*Now*

what?"

"I need to get the key."

"What key?"

"The key to the storage facility where I put the paintings. It's in my car."

"Where's your car?"

"Last I knew, it was at my mother's house."

SEAN HAD ALREADY stopped at the last known address for the former Chief of Police Walter Hobson, hoping he'd find Veronica. But there were new owners at the house who said it'd been foreclosed a few months earlier.

It was inside the Florida State Prison, otherwise known as Raiford, where he sat from the visitor side of the glass and watched Walter Hobson come toward him.

Walter sat down in the gray metal chair, slid it forward and picked up the phone as he leaned on his elbows, looked through the glass at Sean. "Do I know you, son?"

Sean shook his head. "I don't think so. I'm an officer with the JSO, Sean Coyle."

Hobson stared straight at him without moving a muscle. He didn't say a word.

"Chief Hobson, I'm—"

"In case you hadn't noticed, son"—he held up his sleeve—"I'm wearing an orange jumpsuit. The days when someone addressed me as 'chief' are long behind me. So please... just call me Walter."

Sean gave Walter a nod but didn't want to waste any more time. "I'm trying to find your daughter. I was hoping—"

"Which one?"

"Veronica."

He made a face. "She's not in trouble again, is she?"

"Again?" Sean thought for a moment. "She hangs around a kid responsible for kidnapping two women."

Walter took a moment before he spoke, looked behind him at the guard, then leaned in closer to the glass. "Why do I get the feeling this isn't police business?"

"One of the women is my cousin."

Walter stuck his finger in the collar of his white T-shirt under the jumpsuit, loosened it off of his neck. "Me and Veronica haven't been close in a long time. Shit, she hasn't come to visit me more than one time, when I first got here. And I understand she's had some trouble here and there." He squinted his eyes and shook his head a couple of times. "But kidnapping is not something she'd be involved in. I know that for a fact."

"For a fact?" Sean shifted in his seat, leaned with

one arm down on the steel top beneath the glass. "I'll be honest. I'm not interested in going after Veronica. But I'm going to bring the man who's responsible to justice one way or another."

Sean said, "He also killed a man, kidnapped his sister... left a baby girl in the house all by herself."

"Jesus."

"You're right, Walter. This isn't official police business. In fact, they find out I was in here talking to you... I might just be joining you there on the other side."

"You're not a cop?"

"I am. But I was suspended for doing my job... off duty."

Walter made a face, cracked a smile, and shook his head. "Red tape can be a real bitch, can't it?" He looked behind him again, then leaned closer to the glass. "What's the kid's name you're looking for?"

"Danny Womack." Sean could see it in Walter's face, the way his expression dropped. "You know Danny?"

Walter nodded. "You said kid, I thought you meant a boy in his teens. Womack's close to thirty by now, no?" He tapped his temple with his long, bony finger. "He's not all there. I can tell you that much. Veronica'd hung around him on and off for years. I wish I could've stopped it. She always liked those losers, for one reason or another. Hung around a kid, Jimmy, too. The three of 'em. Not sure if Jimmy was her boyfriend or..."

"Jimmy Stanish. He's the one Womack killed. It's his sister he's kidnapped."

"With your cousin?"

"Not at the same time, but... yes. As far as I know, he's got them both." Sean looked down at his hand, the skin torn up from the chain Danny had wrapped around his neck. "I just hope they're both alive."

"I'm sorry, but like I said I haven't heard from Veronica in a couple of years. Last I knew she was working at Raceway selling fried chicken." His eyebrows jumped high on his head. "You ever have the fried chicken out there, the one out by Murray Hill?"

Sean didn't answer, just stared back at Walter. He had a feeling Walter wasn't going to help him find Veronica, whether he knew where she was or not.

But he was wrong.

"I have a daughter... lives up in Yulee. She's got a couple of kids, so don't go crashing in the front door or nothin'. Talk to her... she might be able to help you. Veronica stays with her once in a while. At least she used to."

Sean pulled the Explorer in the driveway of a newer stucco ranch, all garage other than the front door and a small window off to the side. He parked behind a Jeep, the hood up, with a man underneath, skinny like a rail with loose bluejeans falling down off his waist and a white tank top.

The man jumped and whacked his head against the inside of the hood when Sean came up around the front. A wrench dropped and clanged off the concrete driveway. He grabbed the back of his head and bit his lip. "Shit, man." He stepped off a cinder block and looked Sean up and down. "Who the hell are you?"

"Sorry about that," Sean said. "Didn't mean to startle you." He looked at the house. "I'm looking for Veronica? She here?"

The man crouched down and picked the wrench up off the ground, held it clenched in his hand. "She's not here."

Sean's eyes went to the wrench. He wondered if the young man would swing it his way. "She's not here right *now*? Or she's not here at all."

The skinny man shifted his feet, the wrench still gripped tight in his hand. "You still haven't told me who's askin'?"

Sean looked away for a moment, then pulled his sunglasses down off his head. "I am." His eyes caught the wrench shift in the man's hand, starting to come up toward him. But Sean reached for a can of WD-40 on top of the Jeep's fender and sprayed it in the man's face.

The wrench dropped and again clanged off the concrete. The man screamed, hunched over with his hands rubbing on his eyes. "I can't see! My eyes are burning. I can't see!"

Sean grabbed him by the back of his shirt and spun him around, slammed him up against the Jeep with the tank top twisted and bunched in both of his hands. Sean clenched his teeth, his face so close to the man's, he could smell the WD-40 and cigarettes on his breath. "Tell me where she is, or I'll empty the rest of that can in your mouth."

"You burned my goddamn eyes, you son of a—"

Sean ripped him from the Jeep and slammed him down onto the driveway. He had him by the shirt, lifted him, and threw him down again. He reached for the wrench and straddled the man, raised the wrench over his head. "Tell me where she is!"

The man whimpered and tried to block his face with his arms. "Don't! Please... don't! She's in the house."

Sean got up off of him and threw the wrench onto the grass. He walked up the walkway, with flowers and shrubs, and stepped up to the front door. He didn't knock but pulled open the door and walked inside.

He looked into the room on the left. The only sound in the house came from the TV up on the wall. A commercial played with a lawyer and an eight-hundred number for anyone who'd had hernia surgery in the past ten years. But when the commercial broke and *The Price is Right* came on the

TV, the familiar sound of a shotgun being racked filled Sean's ears from behind.

He turned and looked down the barrel coming through the doorway from out in the hall, the shotgun in the hands of a woman two-fifty, maybe three hundred, pounds. She had one eye closed, the other in the sight. No more than a couple of inches shorter than Sean's six-foot frame, he moved his eyes to hers. He raised his hands. "I'm Officer Sean Coyle. I'd like you to put down your weapon."

Veronica didn't budge. Not even an inch. Her one eye still closed, the barrel was pointed somewhere between Sean's face and chest. "Why should I?"

"Because I'm not here for you. I'm here because I need your help. And I'll do all I can to see to it you're not in any kind of trouble."

"If you're a cop, then why aren't you in uniform?"

Sean hesitated, then looked past Veronica. He expected the skinny man to walk through any second.

"I'm looking for my cousin. Her name's Gracie."

Veronica opened her eye and lifted her head from the gun. "Are you Sean?"

He nodded. "Yes, ma'am."

She closed one eye again and put the other behind the sight. "What makes you think I know anything about your cousin?"

Sean took a step closer to her, his hands still raised. He tried to look her in the eye. "Veronica, why don't you put that gun down. We can talk." He showed his hands, glanced at her finger on the trigger. "I'm not armed. I mean, I have a weapon but it's put away. Please. I just want to talk."

The front door opened, and the skinny man walked up behind Veronica. For a split second she turned to look, and Sean grabbed the barrel of the shotgun and tried to twist it from Veronica's hands.

But her finger was caught in the trigger. She tried to pull it back and a shot fired right past Sean's ear, hit the TV on the wall and exploded with sparks and glass falling to the floor.

He pulled the shotgun from her hands and threw it behind him, pulled his SIG Sauer from his pants and held it on Veronica.

Without a word, the skinny man turned and ran out the front door. It slammed shut behind him. Sean looked out the window and watched him run across the grass and disappear down the street.

"He with *you*?"

Veronica shook her head. "My sister's boyfriend. We call him 'the weasel.'"

Sean cracked a slight smile and tucked his gun back in his pants. "I meant what I said, Veronica. I'm not here for you. I need to find Danny Womack. Cops in three counties and two states are looking for him right now without much luck. And like I said, you play straight with me, without any games... I'll see to it they go easy on you."

Veronica had her eyes down on the floor. And when she lifted her head, she had tears in her eyes. "Your cousin is pretty cool. I actually talked to her a bit when Danny wasn't around. I swear, I wanted to help her. Nobody wanted to be involved with something like that."

39

DANNY LOOKED DOWN at the gas gauge, saw the needle down near E. "Why didn't you and Curtis get gas?"

Carla turned to him from the passenger seat. "You told us to hurry."

He pulled the Suburban off Route 40 and turned into the Sunoco, pulled up in front of a pump. He turned to Carla. "You got a credit card?"

She reached in her pocket and held out a card. "Not sure how much is left on it."

He nodded past her, toward her door. "Go ahead, put what you can in the tank."

She kept her gaze on him for a moment, then pushed open the door and stepped out of the Suburban.

Danny turned in the seat and looked back at Gracie. "We better not drive all the way down to your mother's house, find out the key's not there."

He straightened out, looked at her through the rearview. "You sure you only got one key?"

She nodded, turned, and looked out the window at Carla pumping gas. "I don't know why it wouldn't be there. Unless someone went through my car."

Danny still had his eyes on her through the mirror. "Sheriff's office coulda gone through it." Danny stared straight ahead at the sign above the building. It said Food and Gas. "They'd let you in, you know... without a key." His eyes went to the mirror. "You got an ID on you or somethin'?"

She shook her head. "You didn't give me much time to get my things together when you abducted me."

"Will you stop saying *that*?"

"Saying *what*?"

"Abducted. I just don't like that word." He turned and looked back at Gracie from over his shoulder. "We don't have time to drive all the way down your mother's house, find out there's no key."

"I don't think they'll let me in the unit without my license or the key. So we don't have much choice."

The passenger door opened, and Carla stepped back inside, stared straight ahead without a word.

Danny turned the key and started the engine. His eyes went down to the gauge. "You fill it up?" He watched the needle move up toward full before she answered. He shifted into drive and pulled back out onto 40.

After a couple of miles, Danny looked straight ahead and saw the blue lights come up over the hill on the other side of the road from the opposite direction. "Shit." He glanced at Carla and twisted both hands on the steering wheel. His heart pounded so hard he thought he might end up having a heart attack and die... just like Jerry.

He looked down at the speedometer, then looked straight ahead at the road. The sign for 95 was up ahead on the right as the four cruisers, blue lights spinning, buzzed past them headed west, toward Folkston.

Danny let out the breath he'd been holding and felt Carla's eyes on him.

She said, "You think they're heading to your cousin's?"

He looked up in the rearview, made sure none of them had turned around before he answered. He turned to Carla. "Call Wayne and let him know." With his eyes back on the road, he shrugged then gave her another look. "I guess Curtis didn't find Maggie."

"What's his number?"

"Wayne?" He shrugged. "Hell if *I* know." He looked down at the seat between them. "Where'd you put my phone?"

"I didn't touch your phone."

"Well, shit, find it. His number's in there." He lifted himself from the seat and felt around underneath. His eyes were down, off the road.

Carla screamed, "*Danny!*"

He looked up and cut the wheel, swerved just as the tires hit the dirt on the side of 40.

Gracie yelled from the back seat. "You're gonna get us all killed."

He shifted himself in his seat and turned to Gracie. "My phone back there?"

She shook her head. "No."

"Shit, I bet I left it back at Wayne's." He gave Carla a quick glance. "Call Curtis. Let him know there's trouble heading their way."

Carla tapped the screen on her phone. Not a moment later, a phone rang somewhere inside the Suburban. But not Carla's.

It was Curtis's phone. The one she'd just dialed.

Danny reached down into the pocket on the door, came up with the ringing phone. "For someone who's supposed to have the brains..." He looked at the phone, saw Carla's face on the screen with it still ringing, then tossed it on the floor. "They're on their own."

Route 17 was just about a mile ahead. Danny squinted his eyes, looked at a blue Ford Explorer coming toward them from the east. He knew right away who it was and watched as it passed on the other side of the road.

Sean pulled off 40 for gas, pulled up to the pump and stepped down from the Explorer. He turned and reached back toward the center console when his phone rang.

It was Jenna. She said, "Where are you?"

"Probably best I don't tell you."

"I just got off the phone with a deputy from Charlton County, said they have four vehicles on their way out to a farm in Folkston, Georgia."

Sean looked out at the road. "That's Danny's cousin's house. I'm on Route 40, about ten minutes away."

"Sean, you can't go out there."

"That's why I didn't want to tell you where I was."

"Hold on," Jenna said. "Let me grab this call."

Sean held the phone up to his ear and slid his credit card at the pump, pulled out the nozzle, and unscrewed the gas cap.

Jenna came back on the line. "Folkston Police are already at the scene. Sheriff's office was called in to assist. Turns out Maggie Stanish got picked up by a deputy coming out of the woods, somewhere on 40."

"They find Gracie?"

"She's with Womack and the girlfriend... driving a black Chevy Suburban."

Sean hadn't put more than fifty cents worth of gas in the Explorer but threw the nozzle back on the pump, ran around to the driver's side and was on the move before he'd even closed his door. He looked down at the gas gauge, hadn't even gotten enough in to get the needle off E. "I just passed a Suburban heading east on 40, pretty sure it turned onto 17 heading south."

He squealed the tires and turned onto 40, headed back east in the direction he'd just come from. With the pedal floored, the engine made a choking noise he didn't like.

He still had Jenna on the phone. "I don't know if I can catch them or if they took 17 or 95. Could've even stayed straight, headed out to the coast. But that wouldn't make sense..."

"I'm in my car now," Jenna said. "Heading north on 17. Nassau County's already out, got the highways covered."

Sean looked down at the speedometer, just short of a hundred miles per hour, the old Explorer not wanting to do much more than that. He cut it back to take the turn for 17 then hit the pedal hard once he hit the straightaway, leaned forward over the steering wheel and up ahead caught the taillights of what looked to be a Suburban.

He kept his eyes ahead but glanced down at the fuel gauge. The orange warning light had never turned off. But he kept the pedal to the floor and gained ground on the Suburban. He was maybe fifty yards behind. The engine made the same choking noise he'd heard when he left the gas station.

He jerked the wheel like his grandfather'd done when he was a kid and the gas ran low... shift the gas around the tank. The engine came back to life.

He cut the wheel back and this time pulled into the breakdown lane on the right. He drove up along the side of the Suburban and got a good look at the pretty blonde in the passenger seat. He recognized her face. He knew it was the woman outside Jimmy's apartment, behind the wheel of the Buick that almost killed him.

Danny leaned forward from the driver's side and looked at Sean.

But the Explorer's engine sputtered and choked. The speed dropped to sixty then to fifty miles per hour... then to thirty. And then the Explorer stopped, right there in the breakdown lane.

Sean ran out of gas. He slammed the steering wheel with both hands and looked ahead, watched Danny and the Suburban merge in with the other cars on the road and disappear.

40

SEAN WALKED SOUTH on 17 along the shoulder and turned to look back at the Explorer far off in the distance, pulled over to the far edge of the grass.

He called Jenna and told her he ran out of gas. "Don't worry about me. You have to stop them."

"I just crossed 200, heading north now. But the traffic's stopped."

Sean looked around. "I think I'm a mile or so from Becker. Mac's on his way."

"State Patrol's got 17 south blocked, just past Yulee. But it's stopping traffic on both sides."

Sean heard a horn blow behind him and turned, saw the old Dodge Charger's lights flash when he looked. "Mac's here. I'll call you back." He hung up and ran to the passenger side, pulled open the door and jumped in. "How'd you get here so fast?"

He nodded toward the two-way he had bolted under the dash, wires hanging down from the side.

"Pulled a radio from one of the old cruisers, put it in this morning. I heard everything... figured you'd be in the area. Just didn't expect you'd be on foot." Mac hit the gas and pulled out of the breakdown lane and slapped the clutch a couple of times, catching each gear as he shifted. He gave Sean a look. "Why didn't you call me sooner? Before you ran out of gas?"

"You're retired, Mac."

He shrugged and cracked a crooked smile. "And you're suspended..." He turned his eyes back to the road. "How far up there you think they are?"

"Had to've gone a couple of miles, at least. Jenna said state patrol's setting up a roadblock before Yulee."

"Can't imagine they'd stay on 17," Mac said.

Sean leaned forward and looked at the dashboard, the needle up near ninety miles per hour. The engine screamed. He wasn't much of a car guy but could see why Mac liked driving it.

Mac downshifted and jerked the wheel, passed five or six cars on the right. "We'll get 'em."

Sean leaned forward in the seat and saw a Suburban up ahead. "That's them!"

Mac gave the Charger more gas, and it seemed like no more than five seconds they were right up at the rear of the Suburban. Mac downshifted, yanked the wheel and pulled up next to it on the right.

Sean leaned down to look up at the Suburban's passenger side. But all he could see was a woman he didn't recognize behind the wheel. He looked back at the rear passenger window, and a little girl waved at him, a big smile on her face. "Shit," he said. "That's not them."

Mac slapped his foot down and cut into the breakdown lane, then pulled out in front of the Suburban. He leaned forward on the steering wheel. "I see another one. Seven cars ahead. It's gotta be them." He weaved in and out of the other cars and finally pulled up behind the second black Suburban.

Sean's phone rang. He looked at the screen. "It's Jenna." He answered, "We're behind them, still on 17. The plate is nine-eight-Frank-King-Ocean."

Mac eased up on the gas, shifted up and down with the gears. He tried to squeeze next to the Suburban, but a young man in a pickup truck with an American flag on the bumper wouldn't let them in. So Mac stayed behind the Suburban until they were through the stretch of traffic. "He's gotta know we're behind them." He jerked the wheel again, this time pulled over to the left.

Sean looked out his window up at the driver's side and saw right away it was Danny. "It's definitely him." He put down the window and raised his SIG Sauer, lifted himself from the seat and sat up on the open window. He held his gun out straight, pointed at Danny's head. He yelled. "Pull over!"

Danny turned and glanced at Sean, then ripped the wheel. Sean fell back inside, and Danny swiped the side of Mac's Charger.

Mac tightened his grip and straightened out the wheel without going off the road. "You son of a bitch!" He slammed his foot down on the gas, downshifted and passed the Suburban, jerked the wheel back and pulled in front of Danny.

Sean gripped the handle over his head. "He's got fifteen hundred pounds on us in that thing!" He turned and looked back. "I hope you're not thinking..."

"Not with your cousin in there."

"If she wasn't, I would've shot him back there."

But the Suburban slammed into the back of Mac's car, and the Charger swerved back and forth. Mac tried to keep it under control, but they drove off the road and skidded into the grass. He stopped just before a row of trees.

Sean jumped from the car and saw the road blocked ahead. He turned toward Danny and watched him slam on his brakes.

The Suburban went in reverse, and dozens of cars behind it crashed. Danny drove backwards in the wrong direction on 17 until he slammed on the brakes, skidding sideways. The Suburban went up on two wheels then slammed back down with all four tires on the ground.

Police vehicles were already behind Danny. Florida Highway Patrol, Nassau County, and Jacksonville County Sheriff's vehicles had their lights rolling from both sides of the highway. Officers jumped from their vehicles and ran toward the Suburban with guns drawn.

Sean ran past the smashed cars. Drivers and passengers stepped out, but Sean yelled for them to stay in their cars. He ran with his SIG Sauer raised, then spotted Jenna climbing over the divider from the other side of the highway.

They both stopped twenty feet from the Suburban and ducked behind two cars that had crashed. Sean looked through the driver's window but didn't see Danny or anyone else stepping out.

Two Nassau deputies walked toward Jenna and Sean with guns drawn. "You two... put your hands in the air!"

Jenna pulled her badge and showed it to the officers. "Off-duty officer with the Jacksonville Sheriff's Office." She gave Sean a look and yelled back to the deputy. "Both of us." She spotted another Jacksonville officer not far from them.

He gave her a nod with his chin and yelled to the deputies. "They're okay!"

Mac walked up with a .22 rifle and ducked behind the car next to Sean and Jenna. All three stood up and leaned on the hood of the car, taking aim at the Suburban.

The Suburban's driver's side door opened. Gracie stepped out, and Danny stepped out behind her. He had the muzzle of his gun pressed up against the back of her head.

Sean eased his gun down and stood up from behind the car. He looked past Danny at the officers on the other side of the Suburban. He knew he didn't have a shot. Not without hitting Gracie or one of the other officers.

Danny stared at Sean and yelled, "You want her to live another day? Then you'll have to let us drive away from here without stopping us."

Sean walked out from behind the car toward Danny and Gracie. He stepped closer. Close enough to see the tears and fear in Gracie's eyes.

Danny wrapped his arm around her neck from behind and pulled her close to him, the gun pressed against her skull.

Sean knew it was his Glock in Danny's hand. He raised the SIG Sauer and took another step closer. He had Danny's head in his sight and again stepped forward without a second of hesitation. "Drop the gun, Womack!"

Jenna yelled, "Sean!"

But Sean continued, his arms out in front of him with the gun on Danny. He had no cover.

Danny took the gun from Gracie's head and turned it toward Sean. He threw Gracie to the ground and held the Glock on Sean and held it on him with both hands.

Gracie crawled on all fours and tried to get out of the way.

A shot was fired.

There were screams, and the police yelled for everyone to get down.

The Glock in Danny's hand dropped and cracked against the ground. Danny's chin dropped to his chest. His shoulders slumped, and his body collapsed onto the road between Sean and the Suburban.

Sean looked around. At first, he didn't know what had happened. He didn't fire the shot. He turned, looked back at Jenna over his shoulder. It was as if everything had stopped.

Gracie got up and ran toward him, but he pushed her past him. "Get out of here... get cover!"

Jenna reached out for Gracie and pulled her back behind the car.

Sean walked toward Danny and kicked the Glock out of his reach. He saw the other officers rushing toward him with their guns raised.

Sean looked at the attractive middle-aged woman in the front seat of the Suburban. She held a pistol in her hand. But her eyes were down on Danny.

Sean had his SIG Sauer on her. "Drop your weapon!"

She was frozen. But after a moment she looked up at Sean and nodded. She turned inside and dropped the pistol on the floor under the steering wheel.

The other officers charged forward with their guns on Carla. Sean reached in the vehicle and held her arm as she stepped out without a fight.

She looked down at Danny, then lifted her eyes to Sean. "Did I kill him?"

He crouched down and put his hand on Danny's neck. He felt for a pulse, but there was nothing there. He looked up at Carla but didn't answer.

Two officers stepped forward and took Carla from Sean. One officer read her her rights, the other pulled her arms behind her back and slapped the cuffs around her wrists.

Sean walked to the driver's side of the Suburban and looked inside at the floor. He stared down at the .38 that he knew saved his life.

41

SEAN LEANED AGAINST the trunk of Gracie's BMW with his arms folded.

Gracie walked around to the back of her car and dropped her duffle bag on the driveway. "Do you think Carla will go away for a long time?"

Sean stared back at her for a moment before he answered. He shrugged. "It's not up to me how long... but she probably saved my life." He gave Gracie a nod. "Yours too."

She pulled her sunglasses off her eyes and pushed them up onto her head. "What about Veronica?"

He looked out at the street. "There'll be some charges against her, but there's not much proof of her actual involvement, other than her relationship with Jimmy and whatever she had with Danny." He paused a moment. "Unless you decide to tell them more than you already have?"

Gracie didn't answer.

"If it wasn't for Veronica, we wouldn't have known where you were."

She nodded, slid her sunglasses back down over her eyes, and stretched her arms out for Sean.

He stepped forward and gave her a quick hug, then stepped back. He looked into Gracie's car. "Oh, and your front window was broken. We think it might've been some kids... no fingerprints. But I went ahead and had the window fixed. Just let me know if anything's missing, I'll look into it. Otherwise, just watch out for any broken glass they might've missed."

Gracie walked around to the passenger side and opened the door. She stuck her head inside. "Kids?" She straightened herself out and shrugged. "I'm sure it's fine. Nothing but junk in here anyway..." She closed the door and walked around to the back, grabbed her duffle bag, and threw it in the trunk. She continued to the driver's side and stopped, looked across the roof. "Take care of yourself, Sean. I don't know if I'll have to come back here for the trial or not, but..." She pulled open the door. "And I'm just being honest... coming back to see my mother might not be in the cards." She looked up at the empty house. "She clearly doesn't care about anyone but herself."

Sean was about to tell Gracie that wasn't true... defend Nora, like he always had.

But he didn't.

Gracie stepped into her BMW and closed the door. Sean watched her back out of the driveway and didn't take his eyes off her car until she turned the corner down the road. He ran down the driveway for his Explorer.

Sean parked facing the chain-link fence surrounding the U-Store-It parking lot in Kingsland, Georgia. He slouched down in the driver's seat and watched Gracie walk from the front office with a key dangling from her hand. He wondered how far she'd gotten from Nora's when she realized the key she had in the glove box was gone. He'd already called the U-Store-It office himself, and knew all she had to do was pay a fee and show her license to get a second key.

He looked through the fence toward the storage units and picked up his phone.

Mac answered on one ring. "Where is she?" he said.

"Walking to the unit, right now." Sean looked down along the fence and spotted an F-150 parked on the other side of the fence, at the far end of the storage units. "Is that you in the truck?"

"It is. Charger's still being repaired." Mac paused. "You coming in?"

"On my way." Sean hung up and slid his phone in his front pocket. He walked around the fence to the front gate, tapped on the keypad and walked through.

Mac and Sean walked toward each other, and both stopped at an orange steel door. Sean tapped on the keypad and pulled it open, walked ahead of Mac and down the hall, with small storage units on either side of them.

Neither one spoke, the only sound the echo from their shoes on the concrete floor. They turned a corner and saw Gracie.

She stood and stared into an open unit, then turned to Sean and Mac. Her eyes opened wide, and she looked back and forth along the hall.

Sean held Gracie's key up with one hand out in front of him. He had the U-Store-It receipt he took from her car in the other. "Looking for this?"

She stared at Sean, then shifted her eyes to Mac and back to Sean. "You took that from my car?"

Sean stopped in front of her and looked inside the empty storage unit. He turned to Mac. "Where'd you put them?"

Mac gave Gracie a look, then turned to Sean. He nodded. "In the truck. Three of them."

Sean folded his arms and stared Gracie in the eye. "I knew you had to've had a reason for showing up down here after all these years."

Gracie opened her mouth, but nothing came out. She shook her head but remained speechless.

Sean turned without a word and walked with Mac

down the hall. They turned the corner, and he could hear Gracie's voice echo off the walls.

"Sean, please. I can explain. I swear, I was just—"

He stopped and turned to her as she came around the corner. "You stole from your own mother?" He shook his head, then continued behind Mac toward the door. The door slammed behind him and they headed for Mac's F-150.

Gracie came out behind them. "Sean, wait!" She ran up behind him and grabbed his arm. "Will you please just listen to me? This isn't how it looks. I swear... my father called me before he died. He didn't want her to have them. He knew she'd destroy them. That was her plan all along." She looked Sean in the eye. "Please, Sean. I was only doing what he asked me to do. That's the truth."

Sean pulled his arm away from her without a word.

Mac unlocked the door and pulled down the tailgate, reached in under the white cab cover and pulled out one of the paintings.

Gracie said, "He wanted them to hang where people could see them. But not here. He wanted them in New York. That was his home. And those three paintings..."

"They're worth quite a bit of money, isn't that right?" Sean gave her a look.

She nodded. "Yes, they are. But that's not what mattered to my father. He was an artist. He always said if you let money get in the way of your art, you lose a little piece of your soul with it."

Sean gave Mac a look, then turned his eyes back to Gracie. "You honestly expect me to believe you weren't taking these to sell them?"

She stared back at Sean, her eyes filled with tears. She looked down. "I don't want anybody to forget how talented he was. He was special. And my mother would never admit it. She disrespected him for chasing what he loved. *She* drove him away. And she'd do anything to crush his legacy... and his soul."

Sean wasn't convinced he should believe her. "So then what was the plan?"

"To take them back to New York. They were going to hang in RoCo. In Rochester."

Sean scratched his head and gave Mac another look. "Mac, why don't I believe her?"

Mac stared back at him, but didn't answer.

Gracie put on a slight smile and reached for Sean's hand. "Because you only ever got the story about me from my mother. You never asked me anything... or even gave me a chance."

Sean swallowed hard and hesitated a moment. He stepped away and looked down along the building, then up at his Explorer. He turned back to Gracie. "Okay then, if you're telling me the truth... then how about we drive up to Rochester together? We'll have plenty of time to talk... get to know each other." He shrugged, gave Mac a look, then turned to Gracie. "You'll need someone to make sure you and those paintings make it up there in one piece. Don't you think that would make sense?"

He didn't expect her to agree to it. The truth was, he still wasn't ready to believe her.

Gracie paused, started to speak but stopped. She shifted her stance. "But, what about..." She looked in at the paintings. "Don't you have to work?"

Sean shrugged and gave Mac a quick look. "I don't know. I was thinking... maybe I'd retire."

If you enjoyed *Danny Womack's .38*, please share your thoughts with others by leaving a review with the store where you purchased it. It would mean a lot to me as an author and to others interested in learning what readers like you think about the book. Thank you!

Please Join My Reader List

I'd like to invite you to join my reader list to receive free stories, giveaways, and VIP announcements when my new books are released. When you do, you'll receive two free books, *Tell Them I'm Dead* and *What Have You Done?*

Visit **GregoryPayette.com/free-book** to sign up.

Books by Gregory Payette

The Henry Walsh Private Investigator Series

Henry Walsh Series Book 1: Dead at Third

Henry Walsh Series Book 2: The Last Ride

Henry Walsh Series Book 3: The Crystal Pelican

Henry Walsh Series Book 4: The Night the Music Died

Henry Walsh Series Book 5: Dead Men Don't Smile

Henry Walsh Series Book 6: Dead in the Creek

~

Crime Fiction ~ Thrillers ~ Shorts

Shake the Trees

Tell Them I'm Dead

What Have You Done?

Drag the Man Down

Half Cocked

Danny Womack's .38

~

Joe Sheldon

Play It Cool

Play It Again

Learn more by visiting **GregoryPayette.com**